forever since an apple

A NOVEL

by ken welsch

Copyright © 2015 by Ken Welsch

Printed in the United States of America

All rights reserved. This book or any portion thereof may not be reproduced or used in any manner whatsoever without the express written permission of the publisher except for the use of brief quotations in a book review.

This is a work of fiction. Names, characters, places and incidents are products of the author's imagination or used fictitiously, and any resemblance to actual persons, living or dead, is coincidental.

Published by Kage Publishing

First Printing: 2015

ISBN: 978-0692450963

Cover Design by Ken Welsch

to jen

1

Peg didn't understand the excitement below the TV set. The sorority girls, had they bothered to notice, would never understand Peg not understanding it. Watching the dichotomy was the perfect complement to my burger. Different realities.

Peg sweeps popcorn kernels that litter the floor, once had to clean vomit from inside the corner pocket of the pool table, and caps off most evenings by emptying her tip jar onto the bar and counting the change. The allure of the reality TV show that had the sorority girls in a boil was lost on Peg. Even if it was a two-hour season premiere.

"What is it they're fussing over?" she asked. "You know about this show?"

Peg motioned toward the sorority girls. She smiled because she likes them, but shook her head because of what I already mentioned. Different realities.

I chewed deliberately and mulled my reply. I could have told the truth, but then why leave Wanishing in the first place? It's all anybody up there will talk about. I had all I could take, threw a couple of days' worth of clothes in a bag and landed in this bar 15 minutes outside of Big Rapids because it seemed like safe refuge. Plus the marquee advertised "Vennison Burgers." I was hungry and some misspelled food sounded good.

Still, I could have gone with the truth, or at least a version that bore a resemblance, something that dabbled in fact but shielded me from the ugly reality. No pun intended. I could have gone with the truth. I wasn't going to be around long enough to be annoyed. Drop the bomb and slide out of there.

Instead, I jawed that venison until it was ground to mush and rinsed it with four inches of beer.

Then I swallowed. And I lied.

"No idea," I told Peg. "It's a new show, I think. I haven't heard much about it."

Jim Gold says people are either running to something or they're running away from something. I'm not so sure. Seems like most people aren't going anywhere. Like the people at the Nerdy Bird. When I stepped through the door hungry for some venison, I scanned the room and was reminded of what Jim had said.

A group of hunters were deep into a game of Pool Ball Poker. Two guys in dirty jeans and dirtier t-shirts battled on the dartboard. An old couple who probably lived in one of the nearby farmhouses sat quietly at a table watching the evening news on a TV hanging in the corner. And a woman with a pile of graying hair – Peg, it turned out – stood behind the bar working a crossword puzzle in the newspaper. I imagine the scene looked remarkably similar two hours earlier. Or two nights earlier. Nobody looked to be running to or from anything.

"Little early, ain't ya?" Peg asked, looking up from her puzzle to greet me.

"Excuse me?"

"Don't usually see any kids from the college 'til last call. Yer about six hours early."

Amused by herself, Peg set the crossword puzzle aside and placed a napkin on the bar top as I settled onto a stool.

"I don't go to college," I said, and it felt strange to say it. "I'm just coming through town."

Peg nodded.

"What can I get for you, hun? Need a menu?"

"No, I'd like the burger special, please" I said, startling her with manners. "And a draft."

Peg scribbled my order and disappeared into the kitchen.

The Nerdy Bird is a wooden cube, a neighborhood bar without a neighborhood, a miracle that defies business logic. It's surrounded by a handful of farmhouses, miles of cornfields and miles more of northern Michigan forest. The walls are wood. The tables are wood. The bar is wood. And on every square inch are decades of carvings. Names or initials are the standard, but if you look close enough you can find a joke or an opinion on world affairs. A few years ago someone notched "Regan sucks" into the bar top. The Nerdy Bird is no house of scholars.

"I'd a bet my tip jar you were over from the college," Peg said, back from the kitchen and pulling my attention from the carvings as she set a full glass in front of me. I took a drink and it was good.

"A month ago you'd have been right. I finished this summer."

Peg seemed happy to learn her guess hadn't been too far off.

"Did you go to Ferris?"

"No, up in Wanishing. GLU."

Peg chewed her gum some more and returned to the kitchen.

One of the hunters began a new game of pool and the break cracked through the quiet. I returned to reading the bar – someone scratched the word "balls" on there – while I listened to bursts of conversation coming from the pool table. The hunters were debating the young college football season. The guys playing darts celebrated the end of a game by sitting and drinking. The old couple never looked away from the evening news.

"So you finished college this summer, whaddja study?" Peg's trips in and out of the kitchen were remarkably quick, her returns silent, and she always managed to surprise me.

"Hmm? Photography. Journalism."

Peg seemed to approve.

"So, what, you take pictures for the newspaper?"

I really didn't want to get into the details. She whisked back into the kitchen, returned a few seconds later with a basket full of condiment containers and laid out a napkin and plastic ware in front of me. I was back to reading the bar.

"So what now?"

"Pardon me?"

"What now? What are you going to do now that you're done with college?"

I lifted my glass and drank.

"Take pictures for a newspaper, I suppose," I said.

"Around here we've got the *Crier*," she said, tapping the issue in front of her. "Comes out every Thursday. I don't know who takes the pictures, but they've got this fella who writes articles, Dan Lester, he's always riling people up with some of the stuff he writes. I get such a tickle out of him."

I smiled, because there really wasn't much else I could do.

"He wrote an article earlier this summer about the mayor and how he's been driving around in a fancy Cadillac that turns out the taxpayers were paying for. Really made the mayor look silly. There's a story in last week's paper telling how the mayor gave the car back. Drives his old Honda now. I got such a chuckle out of that. You folks all set?"

The old couple was standing beside me. The man set the remote control and a $10 bill on the bar. He and the woman left without saying a word. Peg thanked them before bumping the kitchen door with her hip and disappearing again.

Welcoming all at once a waft of warm air, a chorus of squeals and a pack of sorority girls, the door to the bar burst open. There must have been 20 of them, and they filed quickly into the area left vacant by the old couple. The hunters looked on with not-so-subtle interest. As if rehearsed, the girls began rearranging tables to form one large horseshoe-shaped sitting area below the TV that hung dark in the corner. Holding my food in a red plastic basket, Peg swung open the kitchen door to inspect the commotion.

"What in hell's bells...?" she started before stopping to let a smile spread across her face. "Whaddayu girls doing here this early? Is it last call already?"

A tiny girl with blonde hair pulled into a ponytail skipped to the bar and gripped its edge. A wide grin split her face in half, pushing out a pair of cheeks that nearly buried her eyes and nose. A pink scarf draped needlessly over her shoulders, framing the Greek letters on the front of her sweatshirt. Peg beamed a warm smile across the room as if genuinely happy to see the girls, regardless of how fast they talked.

"Surprise!" the little one squeaked, as if her presence alone truly was worthy of celebration. "We were sitting around the house talking about 'Who's Who?'.

Tonight's the premiere, you know, and Marcy was like, 'We should have a premiere party.' Everyone was like, 'Yes, let's do it,' but the TV room at the house isn't big enough, so then Shayna was like, 'Hey, let's go to the Bird,' and everyone was like, 'Omigod, that's perfect!' I was like, 'Should we call ahead first?' but everyone was like, 'No, let's just crash it!' So here we are. Surprise!"

She fired off words at a remarkable clip, bouncing from one topic to another and hardly taking time to draw air. She was tiring to listen to.

"The show starts in a few minutes," she continued, igniting a new explosion of words that she managed to blend with an equally dizzying montage of facial expressions. "Omigod, the TV works, doesn't it? It's on Channel 4. At least it's Channel 4 at the house. It's probably Channel 4 here, too. Omigod, this is so exciting. Have you seen the previews? It's going to be the best. Do you have the clicker?"

Peg accepted the verbal attack with an experienced grin, waited for it to subside and handed the remote control across the bar.

"The TV's all yours, you girls have fun."

The blonde girl shot back to the group, flashed the remote and was applauded as if she clutched an Olympic medal. In seconds, the TV was on and the girls scrambled to find a seat. Peg glanced at me and noticed I'd been following along.

"Just wait," she said, tapping her fingernails on the bar. "Watching them order drinks is a real treat."

Peg finally set my food in front of me. I checked my watch, saw that I had five minutes and went hard at my burger and fries.

"What is it they're fussing over?" she asked. "You know about this show?"

That's when I lied. Peg had no idea.

"These new shows just don't seem real," she said. "To me, it don't get any realer than Bob Barker. Here they come, watch this."

The blonde, apparently one of the leaders of the group, bounced back to the bar, this time with two similarly dressed, slightly taller friends flanking her. She carried a slip of paper in one hand and a small plaid purse in the other.

"OK, ready?" she asked, as if Peg had been holding her breath anticipating the order. "We'd like two fuzzy navels, five Bud Lights, a Sea Breeze, two gin and tonics, one Corona with a lime and one without a lime, and three cranberry and vodkas."

She traced an index finger along the paper as she read, and clapped the list on the bar top when she finished, still wearing a smile that devoured the rest of her face.

"Oh, and three Diet Cokes. Kristi, Gina and Pam are driving."

Peg snatched the sheet of paper and spun to a cash register beneath a huge painting of a toucan wearing a pair of horn-rimmed glasses and a pocket protector. With impressive speed, she hammered in the entire order. I nodded hello to the girls, who were standing just a few feet away. Three sets of teeth returned the greeting.

"That's going to be forty-two dollars and 75 cents," Peg called over her shoulder. "You girls gonna pay as you go or run a tab?"

The three huddled to discuss before the blonde pinched a 50-dollar bill from her purse and placed it on the bar.

"We'll just pay as we go," she said. "You can keep the change."

"Why thank you darling, aren't you sweet," Peg said as she set five bottles on a round tray. "If you'd like, I'll bring everything over in a minute."

The girls, who had been looking over their shoulders at the TV more than they had at Peg, filled every pause with giddy commentary about "Who's Who?".

"Huh?" one of them grunted. "Oh, no, that's OK, you don't have to wait on us."

Peg went about her business of making the drinks. At one point, she had to duck into the kitchen to carve a lime. I was doing everything I could to devour my food and get back on the road, but somehow having the girls standing there slowed me down.

"Are you gonna watch 'Who's Who?'," one of them asked, catching me in mid-bite. I worked quickly at chewing and rinsed with beer, but the gap between her question and my answer was uncomfortable.

"No, probably not," I finally answered. "I've heard about it a little bit though. Looks pretty good."

"Omigod, it looks amazing," the blonde chirped. I waited for her to add more, but apparently that was it.

"You look familiar," one of the others said. "You don't have English comp this semester, do you?"

"No, I don't go to school here," I said. I could feel my food cooling in front of me. I really wanted to eat.

"That's so weird, you look totally familiar."

I'm not sure how I was supposed to respond, so I didn't.

"You need another one, hun?" Peg asked. She was back from the kitchen and pouring gin over a glass of ice.

"No, I'm fine, thank you," I said. "In fact, I'm ready for my check when you get a minute."

As the girls hauled the trays back to their tables, "Who's Who?" was nearing its start. The group's wild excitement swelled when graphics flashed across the screen announcing the start of the show. Its thumping theme music filled the bar and accompanied a sweeping aerial shot of the United States that closed in on the Midwest and roared into the streets of Chicago. The girls gasped to a collective quiet as the announcer's voice burst from the speaker.

"And so the search for one woman begins," he proclaimed as the camera raced between skyscrapers lining Michigan Avenue. "Prepare yourselves for a journey like no other. Ten men are here for the start, battling in an adventure without boundaries, a game without rules. Each of you millions of viewers at home can join in along the way. In the end, we'll have an answer to the only question that matters. Who's who?"

Peg slid my tab on the bar and eyed the show with curiosity. I was fingering through my wallet while peaking over my shoulder at the TV. The hunters were still shooting pool, in a different world.

"Over the coming months, you'll get to know all of our contestants, including this man," the announcer said as the TV screen showed a guy in his early 20s walking along Navy Pier.

"And you'll meet this man." The video blinked to another guy in his early 20s standing in a bar on Rush Street. I was standing next to him.

Peg saw it immediately, maybe even more quickly than the sorority girls. The blonde spilled her drink. They both fired a look in my direction, glanced back at the screen, then back to me. There may have been a small measure of uncertainty at first, but after a second look they were positive. It was me up there. Hurrying, acting as though I hadn't seen it, I flipped a 10-dollar bill on the bar and stood up to leave. It was too late. Nearly everybody at the table had spun and was looking at me, a few even stood and were slowly approaching. I suppose I could have made a dash for the door, but it never seemed like an option. I felt trapped. I didn't move.

"He-e-e-e-e-y, that was you," the blonde shouted as the show's intro faded to commercial. "Omigod, that was you!"

I looked at Peg and felt ashamed. Like I said, I lied. She was pointing at the screen but looking at me, confused.

"What in hell's bells?"

I shrugged.

The sorority girls circled, anxious to get closer.

"O-MI-GOD, that *was* you, wasn't it," the blonde said again. It wasn't a question.

"I knew you looked familiar," one of the others said.

The sorority girls were really bubbling. Nearly all of them stood and most formed a wall between me and the door. To my other side, Peg lurked behind the bar and said nothing, but wore an expression that wanted answers. I looked back at the sorority girls, who were in a frenzy and wanted to know everything. Finally, they quieted to the point that I might say something.

"I'm sorry, but I really wasn't lying," I said, lying again. "I'm not planning on watching the show."

Somebody held up a small camera and snapped a picture.

"Are you on the show?" one of them asked. "Like, one of the cast members?"

"No, I just know a guy who is," I said. "I just didn't say anything before because I'm kind of not supposed to. They don't want us talking about anything that hasn't aired yet."

There was a short pause before one of them blurted, "Omigod, do you know what happens? Do you know how it ends?"

I debated my response for a few seconds, not sure what to give away.

"Most of it. I mean, yeah."

They erupted and drew closer, blasting me with questions. Peg shared in their amazement despite lacking their perspective. Even the hunters, who I don't think had any idea what was happening, had taken interest.

"This is so - weird," one of the girls crowed. "How were you there?"

"Omigod, the other girls aren't going to believe this," said another. "We should call Sandy."

Finally, the blonde took the floor and the others quieted, as if trained.

"So, you really know what happens?" she asked. "I mean, seriously?"

I could have told them everything, but they really didn't want to know. It would have ruined it for them. They've been watching promos and reading teaser articles for the better part of the summer. Up in Wanishing, you can't go 10 feet without seeing an ad, hearing an interview or reading an article. I'm sure the ad campaign didn't spare Big Rapids. These girls are planning to watch faithfully for the next few months; having the ending given away would spoil it for them.

Peg, though, she looked at me a little differently after that. I couldn't blame her, considering I lied. By the time the commercial break ended, the girls returned to their tables and resumed their journey, as planned, but took turns badgering me with questions. It seemed to help that

Peg filled my beer glass and convinced me to stay. As "Who's Who?" unfolded on screen before them, the girls didn't hide talking about me, and wandered by occasionally to gush, especially during commercial breaks. I didn't divulge much.

But with Peg, it was different. For the next two hours, as the girls shrieked with every new plot twist, she stood across from me and listened. I didn't tell the sorority girls much of anything, but I sat there and told Peg the whole damn thing.

2

Apostrophe was balled up on the porch, pressed against the screen door, warming in the sun. I tried not to bother him as I finessed the rolled up newspaper closer to the door with my toe. Eb hovered over my shoulder, anxious to gloat after getting published on the front page. I finally hooked enough of the corner of the paper to pull it within arm's reach. Eb snatched it from me, peeled off the rubber band and held up the page like he was examining an X-ray.

During the spring semester, a sociology professor toured South America for two weeks and Eb got tagged with writing a feature on her trip. He wasn't a fan of the idea. In fact, he hated it, which had become his standard reaction to any story idea that wasn't born in his own head. In nearly a year as a staff writer for the *Campus Telegram*, Eb usually saw his stories land somewhere deep inside, often buried and edited to half their original length. It's not that Eb can't write, he really can. He just usually chooses to write articles that few people care about. His opinion of the professor assignment changed when he learned that another writer had blown a deadline and his story got bumped to the front. He was pretty worked up about it.

"Beautiful," he said to nobody in particular.

Between his words, my photos and an enormous headline, the story, which only days earlier wasn't deemed strong enough to carry the cover, filled the entire front page. Eb looked like a kid staring at *Playboy* for the first time. His eyes glowed as he scanned the layout; I couldn't help but feel happy for him. It wasn't too big a deal for me; I'd had pictures publish front page dozens of times, and not just in the *Telegram*.

"It looks all right, Eb, the photography is outstanding," I said, jabbing for a reaction. "And Shipler was on his A-game with that headline, huh?"

Eb just nodded, still taking it all in.

"Kind of a weak lede, though, isn't it?"

He stuck an elbow into my ribs and mumbled, but wouldn't let me keep him from basking.

"Check this out," he raved, "they bumped up the type size on the byline."

Floating between the headline and the start of the article were the words, "Story by Ebner Franklin". One line below, "Photos by Daniel Evart". It was clear that Shipler and the gang were stretching to fill space on deadline, but I didn't pick at Eb about it. Why ruin it for him? He might have stood in the hallway for hours staring at that page were it not for Apostrophe, who had woken up and was pawing at the aluminum plate on the bottom of the screen door. Eb heard the meowing and folded the paper neatly, royal treatment considering most newspapers wound up littering the floor next to our toilet.

"Sit tight, Ap," Eb called as he rounded the kitchen doorway. A few seconds later he reappeared with a can of 9-Lives and opened the door just enough to set it in front of Apostrophe's plunging face. He nearly ripped a chunk from Eb's knuckles.

"You know it, man, chicken and liver," Eb said, massaging Apostrophe's mangy body.

With Eb as his unofficial landlord, Apostrophe enjoyed a pampering like no stray I've ever seen. The scrawny orange and white cat greeted Eb and me when we moved into the house last year. He was lounging on our second-story porch, the last few inches of his tail jutting awkwardly upward, like it had been broken. We ignored him at first, and eventually he left, but he showed up again the next day, pawing at what would in time become a hole in our screen.

Eb decided that if the cat was going to be around, he needed some food. And a name. Eb couldn't get past that strange bend in the tail, so he named him Apostrophe. He said it sounded more regal than Comma.

Every day since, sometimes in the morning, other times not until later in the afternoon, Apostrophe scratches at the door and meows until somebody acknowledges him. Until a couple of weeks ago, that somebody was Eb. He eventually learned Apostrophe's dining preferences, and started keeping a stack of cat food cans in the pantry. Chicken and liver seems to be a real delicacy, a dish Apostrophe licks clean every time. Another flavor, a beef of some sort bathed in a pool of smelly, brown gravy, doesn't go over as well. On days when Eb knew he wasn't going to be around, he always remembered to leave an open can tucked beneath an old metal bench that sits rusting outside the door. Apostrophe had it made.

Throughout the summer, Eb was usually on the porch when I got home from campus. He wasn't taking any courses, and aside from the little bit of time he put in writing stories for the paper, he didn't work. I'd get home to find Eb holding a cigarette in one hand and massaging Apostrophe's head with the other. Normally, he wasn't even doing anything. Not reading the paper or talking on the phone. Just sitting there, a drift of smoke curling into the heat while Apostrophe napped at his side.

The day his story printed on the front page, Eb finished catering to Apostrophe, grabbed the paper and hurried into the bathroom. Through the door I imagined him combing over every word, searching for any edits that he could argue about with Shipler. That much was ritual, regardless of where the story ran.

"Hey Eb, how long you gonna be?" I called through the door. "I've got class in an hour. You still want to eat?"

The door flung open and Eb stood there, still wearing a faded t-shirt and a pair of frayed, knee-length shorts. A beat up old Tigers cap angled low over his forehead.

"Let's eat."

Summers in Wanishing are paradise aside from occasional week-long blasts of high humidity and sweltering heat. When the temperature spikes, it helps to remember that in a few months a 20-mile-an-hour wind will slice through 10-degree air, cutting into your face and hardening tears to your lashes. Compared to that, 95 degrees of pasty air is a luxury.

One of the more brutal heat waves in recent memory swept through in August. Shade was crucial. Even Apostrophe learned that lesson, and he was sprawled out beneath the metal bench when Eb and I struck out for a five-minute walk to The Snack Shack.

The sun had climbed to the top of a hazy sky as Eb and I sweated our way past the immaculate fraternity and sorority houses and rundown student apartments that line Lafayette Street. The Snack Shack sits at the head of Lafayette on the northern edge of a campus. Eb spoke occasionally of his story, griping more than once about an unnecessary edit. Otherwise the heat kept us quiet. By the time we pulled open the door at the Shack and were greeted by a rush of AC, Eb was cursing that we hadn't driven.

"Hey fellas, warm enough for you out there?"

Scottie was grinning over his shoulder, talking over the noise of a blender. After a series of familiar moves, he spun around with a chocolate shake and handed it across the counter to a thin girl in a white tank top who immediately had Eb's attention. Scottie is one of those late-20-something types who can't pull himself away from the campus scene. He changes his major yearly, finds new classes to take, and now sits about three credits short of getting 18 different degrees. If they offered a major in academic meandering, Scottie would have his Ph.D. At some point he picked up on the fact that Eb and I both worked for the *Telegram* and he never missed an opportunity to remind us of his faithful readership.

"What'll it be...Mr. Front Page," Scottie said, winking toward Eb as he tapped a finger on a stack of newspapers. "Great story, by the way."

Eb enjoyed the ounce of celebrity and asked for some water. I motioned for the same.

"Boy, by noon I guess we'll have the whole staff in here."

Scottie gestured toward a corner booth where Aaron Shipler, Michael Alley and Jenni Schwartz, the *Telegram* editors for the summer, were eating lunch. Eb, who was studying the girl in the tank top as she settled into a booth with her shake, glanced toward Shipler and rolled his eyes. He might be generally harmless, Shipler, but it's impossible to get past his unending desire to be a hard-nosed newsman. Not to mention his pear-shaped physique. The two make for an annoying combination. Fortunately, as a photographer I seldom dealt with him directly, but he and Eb were always butting heads about story ideas, or whether something Eb had written was worthy of publication, and if so, after how much editorial scrutiny. I never told Eb, but almost every time the two argued I silently sided with Shipler. The guy knows his stuff, I'll give him that. Eb and I ordered sandwiches and fries and chose a table next to the three, knowing that eventually they'd find their way to us anyway.

"Mr. Franklin, Mr. Evart, I trust you've read a copy of today's paper."

It's stuff like that that makes Shipler so unbearable. He always speaks as if whatever he has his hands on is the most important thing in the world. This summer, that something was the *Telegram*, a tabloid-sized weekly that eight or nine of us scrambled to fill for publication every Wednesday. Listening to Shipler, though, you'd have thought we were putting out the *New York Times*.

"Sure did," Eb sighed, unsure whether to stay true to his emotions and gloat, or avoid joining Shipler in self-praise. Somehow he managed to do both.

"Nice work on that Brumler feature," Shipler said, serious as could be. "Exemplary feature writing."

Eb's shrug was his way of agreeing.

"Outstanding photos too, Dan," Shipler added. "I thought the whole package worked well."

"Thanks," I said. "Nice layout."

Shipler didn't even pause to recognize the compliment, as if it was a given.

"Actually, I'm glad we ran into you guys, we were just discussing a new assignment," he said. Shipler picked up a French fry and used it to motion toward Alley and Schwartz, the two assistant editors. Before he continued, Shipler dunked the fry into a pond of ketchup and crammed it into his mouth. It wasn't hard to imagine where the pear shape came from.

"We were discussing a new assignment, what do you guys have going on this weekend?"

Eb turned to me with a worried look, and I returned it. I feared another of Shipler's brilliant ideas, maybe something to do with the end of the summer session, which was only a week away. I imagined photos of students loading suitcases and laundry bags into their cars, because that would have been real original. As good as Shipler is, he isn't the most creative guy.

"Nothing planned, you Eb?"

Eb stayed silent, cautious to commit.

"This new assignment we were discussing," Shipler said for a third time, and suddenly I wanted to throw something at him. "They're filming a new reality TV show in Chicago and taping starts this weekend. The show is called 'Who's Who?'. Don't ask, I have no idea. Someone called the newsroom yesterday and apparently a GLU student is going to be a cast member."

Eb looked at me with renewed interest. I have to admit, I was pleasantly surprised.

"Mike, what's the kid's name again? Darrell something?"

"Darren," Alley corrected, thrilled to contribute. "Darren Morrell."

"Morrell, that's it," Shipler confirmed. "Anyway, we thought you two could drive down and put together a real behind-the-scenes piece on these new reality shows through the eyes of a local guy. Eb, you could really stretch your creative legs and write. Dan, it'd be an opportunity to capture some outstanding photography. The paper will cover mileage and hotel room, but you guys will have to account for any other expenses."

The smile that swept across Eb's face a while earlier returned, flaring even wider.

"What do you think, Eb, you want to do it?" I asked.

"Hell yeah I want to do it, can you fit it in with class?"

I nodded and returned to Shipler, who was steering another handful of fries into his face.

"I called down to get some more info on it, had to leave messages though," Alley said while Shipler chewed. "Let's meet in the office this afternoon to go over details."

"Let's say 2 o'clock," Schwartz said, wanting to play a role. "Should only need 10 or 15 minutes to get up to speed. I'm going back to round up some more information, get you a list of contacts, things like that."

"Splendid, it's settled then," Shipler announced, applying his stamp of confirmation to what the rest of us had already accepted. "We'll see you gentlemen at 2. If I'm late it's because I've got a 12:30. In fact, we'd better get running Mike."

Alley, Shipler and Schwartz, or 'ASS' as Eb referred to them collectively any time they dared tamper with one of his Pulitzer-worthy efforts, started toward the door. Eb was finger-drumming the table, the gears in his head already cranking. It had been about a year since Eb joined the staff at the *Telegram*, and for the most part, it was a forgettable experience. Then in one day, he landed a story on the front page and an assignment to go to Chicago. Finally, journalism was paying off.

"Hey guys," he shouted just before ASS made it out into the sweltering heat. "What kind of reality show is it anyway?"

"It sounds like another one of those match-making shows," Schwartz answered. "I don't know the specifics, but what's the difference. They're all the same."

Scottie arrived with our food and I ate quickly. I was looking forward to getting to class and telling Sidney about the assignment. Eb hardly touched his lunch. He was too excited talking about the coming weekend. He'd forgotten all about the tank top girl.

3

    Carroll Burkett speaks through tight lips, as if the skin on the back of his head is too tight. His gray hair is pulled back over his scalp, though not long enough to put into a tail. I'm not sure what keeps it yanked back like that. The pattern of his shirt usually reminds me of an old vacuum bag, and if you ever see him wearing anything other than blue jeans he'll likely be lying in a coffin.
    His appearance aside, the lasting image most students have of Carroll is of his classroom demeanor, which usually does more to confuse a discussion than it does clarify one. He stands in front of a dozen or so students, the standard size of one of his poetry classes, reads a few lines from a little-known poem, and then surveys the class while asking no one in particular, "Why does the writer choose these words?" When nobody offers up a guess, Carroll looks down at his desk and realigns a stack of papers, occasionally peeking up to see if a brave first-timer will dare offer analysis. It seldom happens, and

Carroll just drops the subject as if he himself has no idea. Whether this is by design or not, I'm uncertain, but if the intent is to get students talking about it after class, it works.

Most people schedule Carroll's classes because they're easy. Even Eb got a B-plus once. Carroll, the long-running theory goes, grades less on performance and more on whether or not he can identify you by name at semester's end. It's a great way to boost the grade point average, with only one brief reading to endure at the end of the term. Any style poem is acceptable, and though Carroll cautions against the three-word wonders, he isn't particularly picky about length. All you have to do is write it, read it and be done. If you look as though you've put in any effort, you're practically assured an A.

Carroll was discussing this final reading when I poked my sweaty head through the door after hustling across campus from The Snack Shack. Carroll's classroom is tucked into a small room on the third floor of Briar Hall, a bland cube of Antique White walls and cream-colored floor tiles. Windows overlook a courtyard and beyond to Jameson Hall, which houses the *Telegram* newsroom. Carroll's desk fronts a green chalkboard, on which he seldom writes. The semi-circle of chair-desks facing Carroll's were filled save for one. Remarkably, the empty seat was next to Sidney, and she snickered as I sat.

"Good afternoon Daniel, we were just discussing our final poems, tackling a few of the, shall we say," Carroll paused, searching for the right word, "*concerns* that some have expressed. Anything you'd like to add before we move on?"

I shook my head and Carroll hardly bothered to notice. Eventually he went from shuffling papers to giving a directionless half-hour soliloquy on what our poems should try to accomplish. I caught little of it. Sidney and I were scribbling updates back and forth in a notebook.

"Going to Chicago," I wrote and discreetly shifted the paper toward her.

She scribbled a question mark.

"Assignment for paper."

She drew a smiley face.

It was always that comfortable with Sidney, from the night we met last year. Eb and I went to see a band called Bag of Hate. He and the bass player, a guy named Stelly, were roommates freshman year. Sidney dates the lead singer and guitar player, Kyle. After the concert, we all wound up at Stelly's apartment for an after-hours party. By 4 in the morning, every couch and corner was littered with sleeping bodies. Sidney and I were the last two standing, and I walked her home.

We've spent as much time together as possible ever since. This summer, in particular, it was easier than you might think. If Kyle wasn't playing a show, he was practicing. If he wasn't practicing, he was working with Stelly on the group's second self-produced CD. Kyle's commitment to Bag of Hate left Sidney not only with a lot of free time, but also with a desire to fill that time talking to somebody. I guess I was just in the right place at the right time.

Carroll interrupted our written conversation by engaging the entire class in a thorough dissection of a poem submitted by a student last winter. The poem was called "Ten Past Ben." I'd have never known it on my own, but Carroll explained that it was about a young boy who lived with the burden of having a purplish-gray ghost appear outside his bedroom window every night at exactly 9:10. Carroll loved it. The kid's race to fall asleep by 9:09 was an unwinnable one since he was so worked up about what he knew was coming. It was real heavy with dark imagery and metaphors, all of which the class explored in meticulous detail. Sidney was put off by its theme of childhood fear and she returned to our notebook.

"When?"

"This weekend"

"Why?"

"Reality TV show. Details later"

It went on like that for an hour-and-a-half. Sidney and I spent a lot of our classroom time this summer that way. I imagine years from now, when I think back on my final college class, that's what I'll remember most. Sitting next to Sidney and sneaking in a conversation on a piece of paper.

After Carroll finally ran out of different ways to say very little, he released us into the sweltering heat. Sidney seemed anxious to get to the willow tree.

"How are you coming on your poem?" I asked.

She shielded her eyes with her hand, looked at me and shrugged.

"How about you?"

I shook my head.

"Then I guess we've got our work cut out for us."

"Meet you there in 20 minutes," I said. "I've got to stop at the office to talk with Eb and Shipler."

Sidney winked and smiled and cut toward center campus. I stopped and watched her as she disappeared around the corner of the building and for about a half minute I didn't pay attention to the heat or the humidity or the sweat or anything else.

Eb was standing in front of an oscillating fan letting cool air blow up the front of his shirt as he scribbled in his reporter's notebook.

"Hey D, how'd class go?" He didn't care, I could tell. "You up for beers later?"

I wiped sweat from my eyes and nodded.

"I talked to Schwartz a little bit already," he said. "Shipler should be here in a few minutes. I've got a phone number for this Morrell guy, but I doubt he's still in town. Thought I'd talk with his roommates a little bit, feel like trying to catch them tomorrow?"

"Don't look at me, you're the reporter. I just take pictures."

Eb had become steadily more confident doing interviews over the past year, but he was still uneasy going in blind. He was more comfortable when someone was with him to help get a conversation started. Eb is funny that way. He is the type of person who would be more comfortable being interviewed rather than doing the interviewing.

"Gentlemen, I salute your punctuality."

Shipler's habit of making a grand entrance lost nothing in the heat. Dark circles decorated the pits of his shirt, and his hair was matted to his scalp as if he'd just sprinted from class. But his stride was as crisp as always, business as usual.

"You guys are still on for Chicago I trust?"

I nodded, wondering how our plans might have changed in a little more than an hour.

"Why don't we step into my office and go over some of the details."

Shipler, as editor in chief for two semesters, was the only staff member blessed with an office all his own. The large newsroom includes a couple dozen desks set up in groups of four, each with a computer screen, keyboard and phone. A printer, copier and fax machine sit on a table against the wall. It's a simple, toned-down imitation of the professional newsrooms in which maybe half of the *Telegram* staff members would one day be employed. And like its professional counterparts, an editor's office keeps the leader separate from the staff. The *Telegram* editor's office is small, nothing extravagant, but it boasts its own computer, printer and fax, and just enough space to house Shipler's steadily swelling head.

He lowered himself onto a high-backed, imitation-leather chair behind his desk, doing everything he could to look as stately as possible. He loved everything about it. Eb and I plunked down on two black plastic chairs Shipler had swiped from a classroom down the hall. We watched him check his voicemail, scribble a note as if it meant life or death but was probably a reminder to call his mom, and straighten a few folders that were already neatly stacked on his desk. Shipler was pretty skilled at finding things to do to make us wait. Finally he cleared his throat, confident that the occasion seemed as momentous to Eb and me as it was to him.

"OK fellows, I just spoke with Jenni on my way back from class and she's briefed me on what she was able to learn."

Briefed. Already I was irritated. You'd think the guy just stepped out of the Pentagon.

"As I said earlier, the show is called 'Who's Who?'. Ten guys battle for one girl is the long and short of it. I'm sure some money is involved too, but we haven't heard how much. The auditions took place in a number of cities across the country over the past few months. Our guy, Darren Morrell, was chosen following an audition down in Detroit."

Shipler paused, as if Eb and I needed a few seconds to keep pace.

"What I'm looking for from you is to talk to Morrell, the people who put the show together, maybe some of the other cast members. Whatever good stuff you can come up with. This is really your baby. I'm planning on this being the lead feature in our final issue of the summer next Wednesday. I presume you will have enough time to turn it around by Monday."

He wasn't asking.

"Ebner, I believe Jenni has already given you Morrell's campus number. I've also got some pertinent information on a document on my computer."

Shipler spun to his keyboard, opened a file and routed it to the printer behind him. In seconds, he snatched the page and positioned it carefully on the desk in front of us. On it was Darren Morrell's name and phone number, as well as the name and phone number of somebody affiliated with the show. Simply writing it on a piece of paper and giving it to us wouldn't have been official enough.

When Shipler was done, he took a deep breath, folded his arms on his desk and said, "I guess that's it, any questions?"

Eb and I looked at one another. There really wasn't much to say, and the silence felt awkward.

With that Shipler rose, revealing that the size of the circles beneath his armpits had nearly doubled in the time we were sitting there. As we walked out of his office,

Eb and I agreed to meet at happy hour to hammer out our travel plans.

"Excuse me, gentlemen," it was Shipler, "would you mind closing my door on your way out? Thank you much."

As I pulled the door shut, Shipler's eyes met mine through the glass. He winked at me and gave me a thumbs-up, as if to encourage a strong performance in Chicago.

Some people make it nearly impossible to like them.

4

A brick-paved sidewalk winds among small pine trees and saplings along the western side of Birch Memorial Library on GLU's campus. Thirty feet away from the brick path is a small pond surrounded by cattails and swaying swamp milkweed. Between the sidewalk and pond stands a mammoth willow tree, 40 feet tall and nearly as wide. Its mint-green branches hang thick and heavy, creating a tent over a small grassy clearing that is shielded from the world save for occasional glimpses through the waving branches. Beneath it, just a few feet from students walking, biking and rollerblading to and from class, Sidney and I felt we were miles away.

I separated two branches and ducked through to find her leaning against the trunk, chewing a blade of grass. She was staring up into the tree, lost in thought.

Her hello was a smile.

"Listen to this line," she said. "I thought of it the other night. It's not even a line really, more of a phrase."

She hesitated, as if rehearsing.

"Trip the mockingbird."

A few strands of her light-brown hair were locked up in the wire-rim of her glasses and she brushed them aside. Long leaves from a branch danced above her head.

"What do you think?"

"No idea," I answered. That much wasn't unusual. Most of the time I didn't understand a word of Sidney's poetry. "But Carroll is bound to love it."

In the shade of the willow, we laughed. It was our own world under those branches, an escape from everything that mattered, a study room where we worked on homework that didn't. It was our clubhouse, our private fort, a place where we talked in a way that we wouldn't anywhere else. It was where I learned about Sidney's childhood, listened to stories of her playing with her sisters on her family's farmhouse near Battle Creek. It was where Sidney asked questions about what it was like growing up in the Thumb, and how I wound up studying photography, and what my plans were after I graduated. Best of all, she really listens. That's one thing about Sidney, when you talk with her she soaks up everything you say, as if she really cares. Especially under that willow.

"Honestly, I don't know what it means either," she admitted. "I'm not even sure what made me think of it, I just like the way it sounds. Trip the mockingbird. It would make a great title."

Sidney's is an interesting approach to writing poetry. Take a line that means nothing, make it the title and then write a poem around it. I'm not one to criticize. Every time I tried to write a poem for Carroll's class I struggled to get past the third word. But I had a hard time grasping Sidney's approach.

"So how about you, let's hear what you've got," she said.

"Nothing."

"Come on, you must have some idea."

"Nope, not a word," I said.

She sat up straight and her face drew serious.

"OK, you're making this way too hard," she said, shifting to a cross-legged position three feet away from me. "Let's try an exercise. Trust me, I tried this once and it works."

Sidney motioned for me to sit facing her, our knees practically touching. Her blue eyes twinkled behind strands of falling hair as she looked into my eyes.

"OK, I'm going to say a phrase. You have to replace the weak word, the adjective, with something stronger, something more descriptive."

I nodded.

"We'll start with an easy one, you ready?"

I nodded again.

"The water is cold."

I hesitated, unsure what to do.

"Come on, quicker, no thinking. Just say the first thing that comes to mind. The water isn't cold, it's –"

"Icy."

She shrugged. "Not bad. Try again, but not so literal. The water isn't cold, it's –"

"Frigid."

She giggled.

"Numbing."

"That's a little better."

We laughed together again, childish giggles that filled our space beneath the branches. I would've spent the entire summer under that willow tree with Sidney. It's safe and comfortable under that willow.

"Let's try another one," she said, encouraged by the challenge. "It was a nice day."

To buy time, I repeated the sentence.

"C'mon, faster," she said. "It wasn't just a nice day, it was –"

"It was, I don't know, it was a beautiful day. It was a pleasant day. It was –"

"No, too literal. Don't think so much."

I closed my eyes and scrambled for a word. I could feel Sidney pressing me to find it.

"It was a –. It was a –," I stammered, nearly ready to give up.

"C'mon, it wasn't a nice day, it was a –"

"It was a –. It was a delicious day."

Sidney's eyes lit behind her glasses.

"Yes!" she said, throwing her hands in the air. "See how easy it is? Now, the next time you're working on a poem, just chewing on your pencil and not writing anything, remember that word. Remember how easy it is."

Across the pond, the whirr of a lawn mower sent a gentle buzz into the air to wrestle with the constant hum of cicadas. A group of students walked beside us on the path, carrying spurts of laughter with them. A bike chain squeaked and then faded. Every sound seemed almost dream-like, barely reaching us beneath the branches.

Sidney and I spent countless hours there throughout the summer. She discovered it a couple of years ago when she was a freshman, and adopted it as her personal study hall ever since, at least when weather permitted. She introduced me to it earlier this summer. Sort of as an icebreaker, Carroll led off his class by instructing us to select an object that would fit in the palm of our hand, and describe it using 15 words. No more, no less. Had to be 15 words. Sidney walked me straight to the willow thinking it would be a good source of inspiration. It worked. I plucked a leaf from one of the low-hanging branches and wrote about that.

Sometimes we laid back with our heads at the base of the trunk and kicked around different ideas for a poem. Sometimes we laid there and said nothing. But usually we talked, not about class, but about anything else. Sidney's wordplay exercise was followed by a few silent minutes, and then by soft conversation.

"So tell me about Chicago?" she said, practically whispering. "When are you guys leaving?"

"Sometime Friday," I whispered back. "I'm meeting up with Eb later on to go over the details."

"What kind of show is it?"

"One of those reality shows. It's called 'Who's Who?'. You ever met a guy named Darren Morrell?"

"No, I don't think so."

"He's goes to GLU. He's a cast member."

"When you coming home?"

"Sunday. We've got to get everything turned in by Monday for next week's paper."

A short pause followed, but it was never an uncomfortable silence with Sidney.

"What's new with Bag of Hate?" I asked. "How's the CD coming?"

"Oh yeah, I forgot to tell you. I heard the whole thing the other night," she said. "I love it, it's a lot better than their first one. They're having a release party in a couple of weeks. You should go."

"Definitely. Who knows, maybe I'll cover it. I'll be shooting for the *Mirror* by then."

We were quiet again. The willow tree guarded us from the sun but not the humidity, and a bead of sweat rolled from my forehead.

"Hey Dan?"

"Yeah?"

"The barn was old."

"Man, you never give up," I said, flicking a piece of crumbled up grass at her nose.

"Come on, I'm serious. The barn was old."

"OK, how about this. The barn was," I said, "not new."

In the shade of the willow, Sidney laughed, and I laughed with her. We sat for two more hours, talking about poetry a little, laughing a lot, sharing our plans for the rest of the summer and not bothering to be bothered by the heat. It was, to steal a line from myself, a delicious day.

5

When I was 10 years old I stashed a wooden box beneath my dad's workbench in the garage. The junk hidden inside wasn't worth much, but I kept a lock on it anyway. I can still remember the combination. When I was 12, my parents took my brother and me camping. Our tent was set up on site number 407. And to my high school graduation, I wore a light-blue, button-up shirt beneath my blue gown. There was a rip in the left elbow, but I figured nobody would see it. Some trivial things feel as if they happened last week.

But I swear I can't remember deciding on a career as a photographer.

What I do remember is taking an interest in photography during high school, and my parents buying me a camera for graduation. At first I just messed around with taking pictures, but when I went to GLU the following fall I took a photography course to learn a few tricks. For some reason, which I also don't remember, I stopped by the *Telegram* office later that year to find out about becoming a staff photographer. It wasn't something I considered a career move. Two days later I was shooting pictures of a dorm being built on campus. A sign that read "Future Home of Rodgers Hall" stood in front of a towering steel frame. A group of university administrators wearing hardhats were lined up in the foreground. The *Telegram* spelled my name wrong in the photo credit, but I didn't care. Without realizing it, that marked the start of my photography career. I've just kind of been doing it ever since.

Every assignment was an excursion at first, even the boring ones like that shoot at Rodgers Hall. There was a thrill to seeing my work in print. Over time that luster faded, and assignments lost that sense of adventure. They were just assignments.

"You worry too much, you know that?" Eb said as he tossed a beer can onto the beach and reached for the duffel bag. "Listen, I'm sure some people have it all figured out. Like Shipler. Shipler probably had the AP Style Book put to memory by the time he finished kindergarten. But most people don't have any idea what they want to be. They just wind up being something."

Happy hour had turned into a full evening, so Eb and I turned it into an all-nighter. We loaded a duffel bag full of beer and headed down to the Sands. By 4 in the morning we were feeling pretty philosophical.

"D, my dad sells real estate," he continued. "He went to college for one year and studied accounting, dropped out, joined the military, finished that and wound up selling insurance. He was miserable, but he found out that he was good at selling stuff. So now he sells houses. Last month he sold a place on Lake Michigan for five million bucks."

Eb's face glowed in the light of the bonfire.

"Five million," he repeated, "and in a way it's a total fluke. It's not like he got a degree in real estate selling."

Our chatter carried across the Sands, a small, sandy clearing next to a sharp bend in the Rustic River about a mile north of campus. Trails groomed by the city connect with others that are maintained by foot traffic. They all wind their way through the forest that borders the streets of off-campus student housing and lead to the Sands. Light from our bonfire flickered over the dark, smooth water.

"I know what you're saying, though, D," Eb said. "Sometimes I turn in a story and I think, 'How in the hell did I end up doing this?'"

We sat silent on the beach, listening to the crack of the fire play over the sound of the woods and the slow-moving water. The blinking bonfire showed a serious look on Eb's face.

"You know, this story will probably be the last one I ever write."

I was squeezing handfuls of sand into a small pile.

"You aren't writing for the *Telegram* next semester?"

"I don't think so," Eb said. "Think about it, this story will go in the last issue of the summer. You're graduating and starting at the *Mirror*. In a way it feels like a fitting finale. Plus, it'll free up more time for Orange Cat, so we'll be further ahead when I graduate in December."

Orange Cat Design was a business Eb and I conceived about a year ago. It started off as sort of a Plan B, something to do on the side. As both of us tired of journalism, the concept swelled to more of a Plan A2. The idea was to do it in our free time until it grew to the point that we could quit wherever we happened to be working. We wrote out a business strategy, created a client list, even picked up a small job designing menus for a local restaurant. Eb would take care of the business end and any writing; I would handle the photography and graphic design. While he tried landing a big job for the Greek council, I tried to convince Jim Gold to get us a brochure project for the Wanishing parks and rec department. Those two jobs would nearly be enough to constitute an official start, we figured.

"It would be fitting," I said, breaking a long silence. "Stories won't get much bigger than this one, at least not in the *Telegram*. Might as well go out on top."

With that, we spiraled into visions of our coming weekend, an adventure that would lead us to a new city and a new experience and undoubtedly the entire front page. And we were getting paid to do it. If only every assignment brought that kind of anticipation.

From that moment, I considered our Chicago trip Eb's last hurrah in journalism. And it felt right. I never considered Eb a career reporter. I couldn't imagine him working for a newspaper 10 years from now, the way I can see Shipler doing it. Chasing interviews and digging up stories just isn't part of Eb's personality.

But for the rest of that night, it was. As orange ashes danced from our fire and disappeared into a blanket of night sky, Eb and I were a newspaper reporter and a news photographer, and we reveled in it like it was a childhood passion. We dreamed up sidebars Eb could write to wrap around his lead story, and about the countless photo opportunities I'd discover in Chicago. And we imagined the unknowns. The hotel. The bars. The people.

Eb and I talked about our trip to Chicago until the sky over the trees to the east began its crawl to pink. Our fire had become a slow smolder, our duffle bag was empty, and the world surrounding the Sands was slowly coming alive.

"To Chicago," Eb said, raising his last swallow of beer.

A few minutes later we were stumbling toward the trails. Home.

D. Food, Eb

It was almost noon and Wally and the Beave were goofing quietly on the other side of the room. Provided the Tigers weren't playing, our TV was locked for most of the summer to the channel that shows the old sit-coms

24 hours a day. Sun hammered through the living room window and found me on the couch, and I woke up with sweat dripping from my hair, sand from the beach still clinging to my legs and an awful smell oozing from everywhere else. Eb's idea of a joke is to turn off the air conditioning when it's 85 degrees outside and a guy is sleeping.

His eloquent three-word note was scrawled on the back of an envelope and stuck to my forehead with electrical tape. I imagined Eb giggling as he pressed it to my head. Turned out, it was a good thing he'd shut the air off because I probably wouldn't have gotten up in time for my photo shoot with Jim Gold. Within 10 minutes I was in and out of the shower and racing toward parks and rec.

Jim called earlier in the week to ask if I could shoot some pictures for him. Actually, the pictures weren't for him as much as for a group of GLU students who had dug a bunch of trash from the Rustic River the previous weekend. These guys were great. To prove the spirit of Earth Day extends beyond one day in April, a dozen of them paddled a three-mile stretch of the river and collected whatever junk they could find. They came away with an impressive heap, including some things I never would have guessed were hidden in the river. A toilet, a couple of shopping carts, a few bike frames, the hood of an old pickup truck and dozens of garbage bags full of typical trash formed a mound that sat steaming in the parking lot behind the parks and rec building. For some reason, the guys saw it as a photo op.

I found Jim in his office, his thick fingers rummaging through a file cabinet.

"Danny, how's it doing?" he said, his hand swallowing mine. "Good to see you, man, how's everything?"

"Same old stuff. Trying to stay cool, it's another scorcher."

"I'll tell you what, this is one of the worst summers I can remember, ever. Makes me want to stay in here all day."

The parks and rec building is a modern two-story structure that makes most of the other city buildings look and feel ancient. Jim's office occupies the southwest corner of the second floor, with windows on both exterior walls. Through the south window you can see straight down Lafayette Street to the Freedom Park entrance a block away. When the trees are bare, you can see another quarter-mile to downtown. The other window overlooks the back parking lot, and through it I watched the river clean-up crew recall animated stories of their adventures in garbage retrieval.

In only a handful of years as director, Jim has amassed an incredible collection of memorabilia. His office décor is crowded but neatly arranged, and it tells his life's story dating back to high school. A No. 85 Wanishing High football jersey covers much of one wall. A Great Lakes University No. 91 jersey blankets much of another. A framed *Mirror* front-page replica celebrating GLU's Midwest Conference championship dominates a third.

L-shaped shelves wrap the corner behind his desk from one window to the other, each chock full of photos and trinkets. Shelves to one side hold pictures of Jim's football career. There are action shots taken by newspaper photographers, staged photos of Jim and his former coach shaking hands at midfield, and at least a half dozen team photos. Adjacent shelves hold pictures of Jim and his family. Jim wearing hospital scrubs cradling a baby Jane. Janine pushing Lily on a swing. Jim and Janine standing at the altar. There must be two dozen pictures of Jim and his family. "Me and my girls," he once boasted with more pride than he realized.

"How's Janine holding up in this heat?" I asked, noticing a picture of a younger Janine reclining in a dorm room more than a decade ago.

Jim winced at the thought of his wife, sitting at home in her eighth month of pregnancy. The third – and final, he insisted more than once – Gold child was due on Labor Day, and Jim and Janine were quietly hoping for a boy.

"I'll tell you what," he said, shaking his head. "The girls were both born in the spring, and she wasn't nearly this bad off. You ever have kids, don't have them at the end of the summer."

I smiled, agreeing to something a lifetime away, realizing again how little Jim and I have in common. Twelve years older than me, Jim graduated from GLU when I was still in grade school. By the time I arrived in Wanishing, he had moved on to a new chapter in his life with the parks and rec department.

We met during my second year at the *Telegram*, while I was on an assignment shooting a new Vietnam Veteran's Monument the city had built at Freedom Park. The memorial includes a walking path that winds back through the woods to the edge of the Rustic. It's an inclusion I've never understood, but Jim walked me the entire loop, pointing out many of the project details along the way.

Jim was a defensive lineman at GLU and though he was no All-American, his hometown legend was cemented by his junior season. That celebrity status ultimately helped land him the parks and rec gig. He married Janine a few years later and eventually they had Jane. By the time Lily was born, Jim had climbed to the director position, one that fits him well. He's a good 6-3, 250 pounds, probably not far from his playing physique. Some of the muscle has softened, but he's still thick and strong.

"So what do you say, you ready to take some pictures?" he said, sliding shut a file cabinet drawer.

Out back, the guys looked like monkeys climbing on their pile of trash. I snapped off a couple dozen pictures, way more than I needed but enough to further convince them that what they had done was monumental. They asked at least three times when the photos would be in the paper, then piled into two rusty little cars and sped off.

"I appreciate you coming down here, they're good kids," Jim said as he watched the cars pull out of the lot. Sweat beaded on his forehead and he wiped it away with an enormous forearm.

"Hey, guess where Eb and I are headed tomorrow," I said, pausing for only a second before realizing how silly I'd look waiting for him to actually guess. "Chicago."

"No kidding! A great place, Chicago," he said, excited. "What's going on?"

I told him what little I knew of "Who's Who?" and Darren Morrell. He listened intently, ignoring the heat and smiling at the thought of such a trip. He was bursting with questions, few of which I was able to answer.

"I'll tell you what, Chicago's a great town," he said, returning to memories of a different life. I thought he was going to break into a story about a trip he and some old roommates had taken, but he just smiled at the thought of whatever those memories were and said, "You guys are gonna love it."

Jim does that, lets his mind flash back to when he was single and still in school and never worrying about things like diapers or his job. He wouldn't trade his life with Janine and the girls for anything, but he gets nostalgic quite a bit.

"When you get back, stop by and tell me all about it. We'll pitch some shoes, cook some pine, have a few beers. The girls are in bed pretty early, and these days

Janine doesn't make it much later. We'll have the backyard to ourselves."

I promised I'd call him Monday and started through the steamy air over the asphalt parking lot. As I was lowering into my car, Jim shouted out the name of a bar in Chicago that Eb and I should try and get to. Pulling from the lot, I saw Jim in the rearview mirror, bending over to pluck a scattering of weeds that had popped through the Cyprus mulch.

6

Eb's Cherokee was parked at the bottom of the steps, its tailgate open and his bags already inside. He spotted me from a block away and leaped up on the porch railing. Apostrophe was curled up at his side, and barely flinched when Eb jumped. I rolled down the window as I circled into the lot.

"Chicago!" he yelled, his hair damp with sweat under the blazing sun.

I couldn't tell what he was more excited about, leaving for Chicago or leaving for Chicago a day early.

"I'm packed! Let's go!" he shouted as I crossed the lot. "Where you been?"

"Dark room," I said. "Those river cleanup guys. I thought we weren't leaving until tomorrow?"

"Change in plans. We leave now and you blow off class."

What a strategist. Missing class wasn't even a concern since it didn't meet on Fridays. You'd think Eb would have picked up on that after two months. A half-hour later we were on the road rolling south out of Wanishing, on track to arrive in Chicago around midnight, by Eb's estimate.

Eb had spent the morning rounding up details of the TV show, getting most of his information during a phone call with a guy he knew only as Stuart, one of the show's media lackeys. Through Stuart, Eb made arrangements for us to get backstage access at the theater where portions of the show were being filmed. Eb explained what he knew of the show while tearing at a Slim Jim, answered my questions in between guzzles of Coke and filled me in on our hotel arrangements through the smoke of a Camel Light. That got us about 10 miles.

"They haven't filmed anything yet," Eb explained. "Tomorrow is sort of the big kickoff, some kind of ceremonial taping at the theater. Stuart was real weird about everything, wouldn't answer most of my questions."

According to Stuart, "Who's Who?" will offer a fresh take on what is quickly becoming a tired reality TV formula. Ten mostly good-looking guys, hand selected by the show's casting director, live in Chicago for a few months and battle for one woman. In the end one of the guys wins a pile of cash and celebrity status for a few months. Eb and I spent at least 20 minutes wondering how 10 guys competing for one girl could be considered a new reality TV show concept.

As the tall pines lining the highway blurred past, our interest in guessing the details of "Who's Who?" gave way to the more familiar optimism surrounding Orange Cat Design. Our expectations were growing by the day.

"Hear anything more from Gold about the visitors guide?" he asked, lighting another cigarette.

"Nothing yet, but I think we've got a good shot. I don't want to press him, it's not really his decision. He told me to stop over for a few beers when we get back, maybe I'll bring it up then. How about you, any word from the Greeks?"

Eb shook his head. "No, but they'll come around. Those frat guys have money. Plus that mock-up you built was the juice, especially compared to that piece of junk they send out now. I saw one the other day, it looks like a fifth-grader made it for them."

As the miles rolled past, our conversation wandered back to Chicago and then back to Orange Cat and more than once to the Tigers. Typical stuff. In between, I filled the stretches of silence by tilting my gaze out the passenger window and watching the aisles of pines flash past. Gradually acres of cornstalks took their place, fields of soft green blinking in a sun-washed breeze. The scenery mesmerizes me, even in the southern part of the state where the land flattens. The further south you get in Michigan, the more it starts to look like Iowa, that's what my uncle used to say. I can't speak to it first-hand, I've never been to Iowa. But I'm sure I wouldn't mind driving through it. Since I was a kid, when my family drove to

Petoskey every summer, I've always liked leaning my head against the window and watching the world slide by. Down around Flint I would marvel at the 18-wheelers throwing exhaust at the highway's concrete walls. Within a half-hour the cement gives way to endless seas of green fields surrounding rickety gray barns that seem a light breeze from crumbling. Eventually the roads twist and turn through deep forests, green orchards and twinkling lakes. The difference in scenery doesn't matter much to me. My brother Paul, on the other hand, hated sitting in the car. Paul would whine before we even left the Thumb. But I never minded.

"Hey, did you talk to Corbin? Do you know when you start?"

Eb's question found me lost in a sprawling wetlands. Roger Corbin is the managing editor at the *Daily Mirror*, Wanishing's city newspaper. If it were up to Corbin, I would have left my final poetry class and raced straight to the *Mirror* office. In his mind it was crucial that his photo staff be fully manned, as if something huge might happen in Wanishing at any moment. Corbin is particular about stuff like that. A lot like Shipler, now that I think about it.

"A week from Monday."

Eb smiled his approval, but I could tell he was more concerned with how my quick start at the *Mirror* might impact our push to get Orange Cat up and running.

I was right.

"What we need to focus on, depending on how much time you have," Eb said, as business-like as he could, "is to land some more small projects, like the menus for Ruby's. I'm still pulling for the Greeks and the visitors guide, but to get us rolling we need some quick-turn jobs, build up our portfolio."

Ruby's is a diner on the south side of town, and the first official client of Orange Cat Design. We were redesigning their menus for fifty bucks. Eb had the idea that a bunch of small jobs like that one would be as good, and in some ways better, than one high-paying job.

Eb, it was clear, would be the business mind behind OCD, the informal name he assigned to the company, as if shaving three-tenths of a second from his schedule was crucial. His rank as chief editorial contributor was slowly taking a backseat to sales pitching and number crunching. To help, I had gone through a few recent issues of the *Telegram* and *Mirror* and circled any of the ads that I thought could be improved.

"A few more prospects for us," I said, reaching to the backseat to grab the papers from my bag. "These ads are horrible. Weak designs. Out-dated fonts. Bad writing."

Eb's eyes bounced between the newspapers in my hand and the road in front of us.

"Perfect, we'll go right to them with fresh mockups."

Traffic on M-37 was light, especially in the southbound lane. Oncoming traffic was a little heavier with vacationers getting an early jump on a weekend Up North. Eb had a clear road to push the Cherokee hard.

He was sifting through ideas for Orange Cat in his head, it was obvious because every now and then he'd toss out a thought about a business we might approach or an angle we hadn't considered yet. Then he'd fall quiet again for miles. I was thinking about Sidney.

"Hey D, check this out," Eb said, and my attention snapped back inside the Cherokee. His face lit as we closed on the back of a red convertible. "Look what we've got up here."

Blonde hair was blowing all over the place. The girl in the passenger seat turned and waved. We rode in their wake for a mile or so before Eb veered into the northbound lane and hurried alongside them. Through the passenger-side window I could practically have reached over and held hands with the driver. The girls did their best to look sexy, sipping diet soda, smiling, and rocking back and forth to what I imagined was a horrible dance song. Eb did his best to look cool behind the wheel, smiling casually, nodding in the direction of the driver. I did my best to not look like a moron. I waved, looked at Eb, then at the convertible, then back at Eb. The whole thing was silly. I just assumed Eb would remember we were passing on a two-lane highway.

The horn of the beat up old pickup truck coming at us was 30 yards down the road, but I'd have bet it was mounted to our hood. By the time Eb reacted it nearly was. All in one motion he pounced on the brake pedal and cut behind the convertible, both of us too stiff to let loose any choice profanity. The Cherokee, sliding nearly sideways, dug hard into the pavement before reaching the gravel shoulder and then the high weeds that line it. When we finally slid to a stop, the Cherokee's two back tires sat just off the southbound lane, the front wheels were surrounded by waist-high fescue and the front bumper rested a few feet from a highway marker. I'm not sure how much time passed before Eb and I managed to move. Both the convertible and the old pickup were long gone. With his temple resting on the steering wheel, Eb stared at me in disbelief.

Eb finally reached for the stereo to cut the Nirvana CD we'd been listening to. Our chests heaved behind our t-shirts, and the sound of our breathing filled the car. My face pressed against my forearms, which hugged the dashboard. It was the only time I can remember Eb looking scared. He finally straightened the truck to the road's shoulder, and we stepped out to a warm breeze that carried the smell of manure. Eb lit a cigarette and inhaled hard. We hadn't spoken in minutes.

"Holy shit," was all he could eventually manage, and my silence was agreement enough.

We leaned against the truck as an occasional car roared past, bringing a burst of slightly cooler air with it.

"I thought we were dead," he whispered, exhaling another cloud of smoke. "You OK?"

I nodded.

"I thought we were dead," he said again.

The next five miles were the quietest stretch I've ever spent in a car. No music, no conversation, only the steady hum of tires on the road. I returned to staring out the passenger window, but the passing landscape didn't have my attention. All I could picture was the grille of that old pickup truck closing in on us. Eb was too busy chain smoking to talk. He broke the silence when a sign alongside the highway caught his attention.

"There's our tax dollars at work, D," he said, shaking his head and wearing the expression of someone who had eaten paint. "Did you see that?"

I hadn't.

"It said, 'Do Not Attempt To Pass While Oncoming Traffic Is Present,'" Eb said, shaking his head. "I'm telling you, they think people are idiots."

I tangled with the irony, agreeing with Eb but still rattled from our near-death experience. His disgust was visible.

"They might as well put up a sign that says, 'Don't Drive Your Car Into Another One.'"

It was a comment born of anger, anger at himself I suppose, and I was doing everything I could to bottle up a burst of laughter. Eb finally noticed my grin and his disgust gave way. We launched into a laughing frenzy, alternately offering up equally inane road sign suggestions.

"'If You Think You Are Going To Run Into Something, Turn,'" I said.

That about knocked Eb out the driver's side door. We were entertaining ourselves to tears.

"'Ramming Your Car Into Other Things Is Not Allowed,'" Eb said, wiping his eyes. I was folding toward the floor by that point, and Eb was slumped over the center console. I'm not sure how he was keeping us on the road.

"'Crashing,'" I said, "'Is Discouraged.'"

The car swerved when Eb heard that one. We volleyed various versions back and forth until the Hilltop Tavern, a dumpy little bar somewhere north of Grand Rapids, appeared alongside the highway a half-mile ahead. Eb wanted a break from the truck, not to mention a drink, and I didn't object. As he turned the Cherokee into the pot-holed parking lot I massaged the ache from my cheeks.

Within 20 minutes, the waitress, who wore an incredibly tall mound of orange hair, dropped two cheeseburgers and a basket of fries on our table. Eb swallowed the rest of his beer and motioned for two more. In the back of the bar, a song by Garth Brooks played from a jukebox to greet the farm workers filing in after a day in the fields and orchards. Few bothered to clean off the evidence. Before long the floor at the Hilltop looked like a garden.

A pool table in the center of the room gradually became the focal point of the evening. Guys of various size and age, most of them dressed in dirty faded jeans and t-shirts, threw familiar catcalls across the table. They all answered to what I assumed were abbreviations of their last names. They lined stacks of quarters on one edge of the pool table, and the crack of the cue ball signaled the start of what would be an evening-long series of games played by guys who I imagined had been running together since grade school. Eb studied them as they went through their ritual. Midway through his burger, He caught the attention of nearly everybody in the room when he walked over and set a stack of quarters in line. It seemed like 50 pairs of eyes followed him back to our table.

"Why not," he whispered, smiling.

Orange Pile returned as I stood from the table. Eyes followed me to the back of the bar. The smell of a bleach-and-tobacco-and-urine concoction assaulted me as I entered the bathroom, but a palm full of cold water helped rinse away the nerves that lingered from our close call. My cheeks were still a little sore. When I got back to the table, Eb was sitting quietly, sipping his beer as he analyzed the Hilltop clientele.

"How would you like this life?" he whispered, making it clear that he would pass if given the choice.

"What?"

"Look at these guys," he explained, his whisper wrestling with the country music. "They've probably lived out here their whole lives, been coming to this place since they were 16, don't do anything but work themselves filthy all day, then come here afterwards and get greased."

I smiled and shrugged, neither arguing nor agreeing. Eb seemed bothered that I wasn't as bothered as him.

"It just seems like after a decade or two you'd start to think there has to be something more."

I sided with him on that point, though I wasn't sure what that something else was, nor who could rightfully question whether somebody else should want it.

Orange Pile found her way through the thickening crowd and moved two shot glasses from her tray to our table. Eb stared at me, waiting for a reaction.

"Just one quick one," he said, lifting a glass while motioning me toward the other.

"What is it?" I asked.

I didn't really care.

"Jack. Come on, we both shoot better after a few drinks."

We winced as the whiskey went down, agreeing without saying a word that Chicago could wait one more night.

7

Last semester, Eb heard about a closed party at the Sigma Tau Epsilon frat house. We normally stay away from Greek parties, especially invite-only ones, but he'd been after a girl who was a Delta Tau, one of the sororities on the list. He talked me into going with him. We managed to slip into the house through a side door and blend with the crowd for a while. A couple of hours later, Eb was behind the bar working the keg, controlling the stereo. If you'd have wandered into the place, you would have thought Eb was hosting the damn party. He does that kind of thing all the time.

He did it again at the Hilltop.

A little after midnight, Tom McGinnis and Russ Jiminski stumbled toward our table and motioned Orange Pile for a round of beers. They were Hilltop regulars and they seemed almost thankful for the intrusion of two college kids. Eb and I called them Mac and Jimmer because everybody called them Mac and Jimmer.

"What's up CB?"

Our nickname at the Hilltop was College Boy. It didn't matter which of us they were talking to. Mac came up with the clever abbreviation.

"You guys here for the night?"

"Neither of us is driving anywhere," I said, motioning toward Eb, who had been recruited to play a game of doubles.

Mac and Jimmer settled into chairs at the table with me. The twang of a steel guitar filled the room.

"Well, welcome to the Hilltop," Mac said, a greeting that came hours after our arrival. We drank to it anyway.

"How did you guys wind up here, anyhow?" Jimmer asked. "Long way from Wanishing."

I told them about our trip to Chicago and about "Who's Who?" and about working for the newspaper and about how Eb and I had nearly gotten creamed on the highway. They seemed genuinely interested in every detail, pulled into a world so far from their own that they raked me with questions.

"A photographer, huh?" Jimmer asked. "Must be pretty cool, working for a newspaper and all."

"It's not bad. Assignments don't usually take us to Chicago, but it's OK."

Mac's face turned redder with every beer. By midnight it beat like an uncomfortable sunburn.

"Hell, Jimmer used to practically own the *Argus*," he said. "Second team all-state pitcher. Carried us to the finals."

Jimmer seemed reluctant to join Mac in raving about his high school glories. Mac prodded him with the story of a one-hitter Jimmer threw in a regional final, but Jimmer stayed quiet. Mac didn't seem to mind providing the color commentary himself.

"Lost in the state finals, 4-2. We shoulda had 'em. Shit, we did have 'em, 'til Jimmer's arm blew. Just one pitch and 'Snap!' He couldn't a raised his arm to wipe his nose on his sleeve."

As Mac's narrative rolled along, Jimmer gazed through the neon curves decorating the window, working the label of his beer bottle with a fingernail. The heavy thump of a rap song took the place of country music and filled the Hilltop's walls. Jimmer's smile had faded.

"We're up 2-0 in the sixth," Mac continued. "Jimmer was dealing, they couldn't touch him. I was playing first base, I could tell the minute he let go of the ball that something wasn't right. His arm just hung there."

Jimmer, who looked older than his mid-20s with a tanned but weathered face and thinning, sun-bleached hair, was deep in thought while he listened to the story, no doubt hearing it for the thousandth time. He glanced occasionally at Mac's animated way of reliving the memory.

"This was the championship game?" I asked.

Jimmer turned his eyes to me and nodded, then returned them to the backside of the neon sign.

"Junior year, last game. Shit, it was the second to last inning," Mac said. "Four outs away. Jimmer's working on a two-hitter, and both of them were little infield dribblers. I'm telling you, they couldn't touch him. Nobody could touch him all season."

Mac stood to demonstrate the final pitch, then plopped back into his chair and swallowed deep from his beer.

"His arm just fell. I knew right away. Second team all-state, done like that."

Mac snapped his finger for emphasis, and Orange Pile mistook it for a rude way of ordering another round.

"You drunk bastard, I'll be there when I get there," she cackled from a nearby table as she wiped a handful of crumbs to the floor.

Mac nearly fell out of his chair laughing, drunkenly started to explain that he wasn't calling for her, and then decided the easy way out would be to let her bring the beers. She appeared a minute later with three bottles.

"Thought I was gonna die of thirst," Mac said, trying to hold a straight face. "If I'm gonna want another one, should I order it now?"

Orange Pile glared at him like he was manure.

"You keep on me like that and you best get to a different bar if you want another one."

She stormed off and we all laughed, though none as deep as Mac. Once the laughter faded, he returned to his story like he had bookmarked it.

"Anyway, we had big pictures and stories about us all season in the *Argus*. Undefeated all year. Seems like at least half the time it was a picture of Jimmer. We were the Golden Arrows, so the headline usually said something like, 'Golden Arm' or 'Targeting a Title.'"

You could tell by the way Mac glowed that those days were life's highlights.

"After we lost in the final, they put a big picture on the front page of Jimmer standing on the mound, his arm hanging to the side. The headline said, 'Broken Arrow.'"

Jimmer's eyes were fixed on the center of the table, his mind back on that mound.

"It was one hell of a run," Mac said as he reached his beer across the table. The two tapped bottles before Jimmer stood and staggered to the bathroom.

Mac wobbled in his chair, held his bottle across the table a second time and said to nobody, "A hell of a run."

"Jimmer ever play again, in college or anything?" I regretted asking it before it was even past my lips. Mac wasn't upset by my asking, he just shook his head, still reliving the disappointment.

"No, and that arm coulda got him somewhere," he said. "Scouts were at our games all season whenever he pitched. Pro scouts, college scouts, you name it. He was leaning toward Eastern. Probably woulda been drafted too, that woulda changed everything. But he couldn't play anymore. Could never throw the same after that."

We sat quietly for a few seconds when a loud roar from the pool table broke our silence. Eb sunk an eight-ball bank shot and was greeted by a swarm of cheers and high-fives. Even the guys he'd beaten were shaking their heads and smiling as they pulled wads of one-dollar bills from their pockets.

Eb's celebration carried to our table, and Mac thumped him on the bicep with a congratulatory fist that was sure to bruise. Eb wasn't fazed. He was greased.

We were just two more guys in the crowd, not feeling a bit out of place. We shot pool, played the juke box, drank beer and traded stories with people we'd never met but in a way felt we had known for years. By closing time, Eb had started to fall asleep at the table, his forehead bobbing in a losing fight to stay awake.

I pulled the Cherokee to the back parking lot while Mac and Jimmer helped get Eb out the door. They steered him into the passenger seat and Eb was asleep instantly.

I curled up in the backseat, my head pressed against a duffel bag, a sweatshirt draped over me for a blanket. As I looked up and out the window of the car, I could hear the crowd from the Hilltop as they stumbled to their cars.

And then it was quiet. Completely silent except for a car zipping past on 37 every few minutes. I laid awake for probably a half-hour looking at the stars sprinkled across the darkness, and thinking. Night time is always the best time for thinking. I thought about Chicago and wondered what Eb and I had waiting for us. I thought about Jimmer and his golden arm hanging limp. For a few seconds, I thought about the poem I was supposed to be writing. But more than anything, as I laid there and felt myself fall into a deep sleep, I thought about Sidney. Sidney would have had a blast at a place like the Hilltop. She really would have liked Mac and Jimmer and all the people we met.

And, man, they would have loved her.

8

"D, you're missing it man. You gotta see this."

Eb called to me as he slowed the Cherokee to the shoulder of the freeway. Sun pounded through the window and into the back seat, a blinding brightness that forced my face back into the duffel bag.

I felt the truck come to a stop, and heard cars rumble past as Eb paused before opening the door.

"D, come on, you gotta check this out. We're here."

The door slammed shut and I wondered for a minute where "here" was, but my eyes wouldn't open to the sun beating through the windows. The last thing I could remember was laying in the back seat in the parking lot behind the Hilltop, staring out the window at the stars, listening to Eb's deep breaths from the front seat. I struggled to open my eyes while my head pounded behind them. From the back of the truck, the windshield started as a solid wall of yellow before slowly the picture came into focus. Eb was leaning against the right side of the hood, smoking a cigarette as he appraised the scene in front of him. The towers of Chicago, mammoth gray buildings against a cloudless blue sky, stood maybe three miles ahead.

Eb walked around the passenger side and leaned in toward the rear window, rapping his knuckles against the glass. I shielded my eyes and looked at him so he'd know I was awake.

"You see this?" he called through the window. "Come on, grab your camera."

I managed to pull myself upright and climb from the truck, joining Eb on the shoulder of the highway. He stared almost proudly at the Chicago skyline as a semi thundered past.

"Is that awesome or what," he said, still soaking up the city. "I knew you wouldn't want to miss this."

He was right. Chicago spread before us with unimaginable potential. We had no idea what to expect and, as a result, we expected everything. Standing by the side of the highway, I felt waves of warm air from the passing traffic, and with each car that passed, a jagged remnant of the previous night went with it. My head began to clear as I scanned the city, wondering as I looked through my camera lens which tower in this mass of buildings was our hotel.

"We're here, man," Eb repeated. "Come on, let's go."

Eb had us back in traffic in no time, and he navigated the foreign streets of Chicago with remarkable familiarity.

He occasionally referred to a piece of paper on which he had scribbled some directions.

"What time did we leave this morning?" I asked, still wiping my eyes awake. "Sorry I left you to drive alone all morning."

"No problem, it was an easy drive. I woke up at about 7, the sun was just hammering me in the front seat. I popped right awake and once I did I figured I'd get us on the road. We flew. Hardly anyone on the road until we got out of Michigan."

Eb figured we had plenty of time to find the hotel, get checked in and then wander around for a while before it was time to get to the Clark Theater. Filming was scheduled to start that afternoon, and though Eb wasn't sure exactly what they were filming, Stuart had made it clear that it was an important day on the show's production schedule. Reporters antsy for a behind-the-scenes look were coming in from all over the country. Eb and I were giggly as we wound our way through the city in search of the Ashton Hotel. We'd never been so close to fame.

Every strand of Darren Morrell's sandy brown hair was positioned with purpose, but the stylist tinkered with it for another 15 minutes anyway. A make-up artist brushed some kind of powder on his lightly tanned face.

Someone else leaned over and plucked a few hairs from his nostrils. When it was agreed upon that Darren was fit to be televised, he sat straight and studied himself in a mirror.

"That part I'm going to have trouble getting used to," he sighed, stepping from the barbershop-style chair and peeking one last time at the reflection of his new face.

I was snapping pictures. Eb was scribbling in his notebook. Darren was doing his best to hide looking scared. Taping was less than an hour away and the Clark Theater was buzzing with final preparations. The small, two-story brick building tucked quietly within Chicago's theater district, hiding in the shadows of the skyline towers we had gazed at from the highway, had been transformed from a dirty-bricked community theater to, as Stuart put it, "one that would more adequately provide the modern feel that we'd like to project." Whatever that meant. Near as I could tell, it meant they'd use a lot of black curtains as backdrops.

Eb and I hustled through lunch at a deli and found our way to the theater two hours before taping. Stuart was kind enough to break from his hectic pre-shoot schedule to give us a quick tour of the theater. From a tiny room that served as his office, he led us down a dark hallway, somewhere backstage.

"I'm glad you guys made it down, a little pre-pub never hurts," he said. "By the way, did you sign the release forms when you came in? Certain info is restricted until we go live, for obvious reasons."

The reasons weren't obvious to us, but Eb and I nodded anyway, holding back our laughter. It wasn't easy. Stuart, or Stu as he insisted, reminds me of a sci-fi creature. He stands about 5-foot-2, and his jet-black hair points two inches from the top of his head, thick with a hardening gel. A weak attempt at sideburns make the sides of his face look dirty, and a pair of glasses with lenses thick as a windshield nearly double the size of his eyes. He's a nice enough guy, but almost impossible to look at.

"All right guys, here's the deal," he said, leading us onto the main stage where the bulk of the day's taping took place. "After we leave the stage, don't come back up here, at least not until the taping is done. You guys can sit anywhere out in the seats if you want to watch; that's where the other journalists will be. Dan, they told you no photos during taping, right? OK, any questions so far?"

Eb looked confused, as if expecting a bit more direction. I couldn't blame him.

"Can you tell us a little bit about the show?" I asked. "How is this whole thing going to work?"

"Actually, I can't tell you that much, but what do you want to know?"

"What's the set up?" Eb asked. "I know there are 10 guys and in the end one of them gets matched up with a girl. But how?"

"Can't tell you that," Stuart said shaking his head.

"Why not?"

"Can't tell you that either. Even the guys on the show don't know. Let's do it this way. Why don't I tell you what I can, and we'll go from there."

I didn't mention Stuart's teeth. His canines on the top are huge, and when he talks they hang like fangs in front of his lower lip causing him to whistle his S's. Believe me, it's a real challenge to have a conversation with him.

"Here's what's happened so far. These guys were all nominated last spring, by a friend, a co-worker, whoever."

Eb and I nodded.

"After looking at some videotapes, running some auditions, we broke the list down to these 10."

We knew that too.

"The guys all agreed to be part of the show knowing only this; that the 10 of them will compete to win 250 grand."

That much was news. Eb whistled as he jotted the info in his notepad.

"What about the girl?" he asked. "Isn't there the chance to meet your dream girl, that whole thing?"

"To that I can only say yes, and nothing more."

"Will the woman, or women, be here today?" Eb pressed.

"Can't say."

Stuart really loved possessing information that was in demand. Eb was getting tired of asking questions and not getting answers, and Stuart seemed to notice.

"Let's see, what else can I tell you? Taping will take place here in Chicago, I can tell you that much. Umm, that's about it though."

Eb and I must have looked confused as hell, because Stuart started with an explanation without either of us asking for one.

"Here's the deal, guys. Most of the questions you've asked will get answered when taping starts. This whole thing's been set up that way. We want these guys to first learn all of the details in front of the cameras, to get genuine reactions on tape. Then you'll see the same treatment in the promos before the show airs – a lot of questions, not many answers. That's why you guys had to sign those consent forms, agreeing not to divulge certain info."

Stuart seldom stopped to breathe adequately, and once he got rolling his pauses were brief, allowing him only a second to pull in as much air as he could.

"You'll see some heavy advertising within a week or two. The show premieres the day after Labor Day, and by then it's going to be an all-out blitz. But all of the promos are going to play up the mystery factor, getting people wanting to watch without really knowing why. When that first show airs, the producers want to make sure viewers are surprised. And to do that, they want the cast to be surprised. And I mean genuinely surprised. These guys aren't actors. It's gotta be real."

It made more sense to Stuart than to us, but we accepted it. Having sensed that we were satisfied, Stuart led us backstage, down another dark hallway that split from the one we'd come in through, to a dressing room in the back of the theater.

"The guys are getting ready, you should find Darren in here. If not, he's probably roaming around the theater or out grabbing a smoke. There are a lot of pre-show jitters going around."

We thanked Stuart, shook his hand, and watched him hurry down the corridor back toward his tiny office. Before he disappeared around the corner he stopped, glanced over his shoulder and called, "Hey guys, trust me. Come September, this is gonna be frickin' awesome."

Darren was getting worked on as Eb and I eased the door open. A stylist with more nose rings than nostrils asked who we wanted, then tipped her head to the next chair.

"Ebner, is that you?" Darren asked, staring stiffly at us through the wall mirror. "Glad you made it. Give me a few more minutes here, I'm just about done."

The hair, the powder, the nose hair plucking, it all took forever, but made for a great photo opportunity. When it finally ended, Darren was anxious to walk off some nerves and he motioned us to follow.

"I've never been a big fan of cameras," he admitted, glancing at me. "I guess I'd better get used to them or it's going to be a long couple of months."

A few of the contestants with similar model good looks were still in chairs that lined the mirrored wall of the make-up room. A handful of others had already been primped and were milling around the theater looking for ways to burn nervous energy. In the hallway, a camera crew waiting to capture backstage footage slowed Darren by asking him questions about his expectations for the show, then followed him down the corridor. Eb and I did what we could to avoid invading the frame.

Darren, who must have looked like royalty with us trailing, led us to an area off the right side of the stage. Camera crews and light and sound techs were setting up equipment while stagehands hustled to put the finishing touches on the set. It was here, Darren guessed, that much of the first episode would be filmed.

"I kind of want to get a look at these girls, know what I mean?" Darren said, raising his eyebrows.

We knew what he meant.

"Hey, about that," Eb asked quietly, as if keeping a secret. "How much did they tell you guys about the show? How many girls are there?"

"They didn't tell us anything. That's what makes this so scary. They told us we'd be here for a month for sure, maybe longer. And they told us the winner gets a quarter-million dollars. Seriously, that's about all they said."

"So what's going through your mind now?" Eb asked, playing the role of reporter for a few minutes. "Starting to regret it, or are you just nervous?"

Darren studied the theater ceiling and dried his palms on his thighs. Eb was ready with his pen.

"Ebner, you have no idea."

9

Thad McCormick looks like a news anchor except younger. He was dressed in a black tuxedo. His light brown hair covers his skull like a helmet. His skin is tanned, like that of nearly anybody else at the Clark Theater who might wind up on camera. Long, feminine lashes flutter in front of his light blue eyes, and a dimple sinks about three inches into his chin. He is the type of guy you might expect to be doing something like hosting a reality TV show. That dimple, it's like somebody drove a nail into his face.

All eyes were on Thad well before the lights dimmed and taping of "Who's Who?" finally began. Months of preparation led everybody in the theater to this point, and nervousness filled the auditorium. Even I, who had no vested interest in what was happening, could feel it. To the side of the stage, Stuart and the others who'd been scurrying around all day making sure everything ran smoothly, finally were able to take a breath and watch the drama unfold. Moments before the lights dimmed, Eb tugged on the sleeve of a 21-year-old cast member from Los Angeles and asked, "What's it feel like, finally getting to this point?"

The kid thought for a second.

"It's just totally awesome, man," he said, struggling to find appropriate words and failing. "It's like – man, it's just awesome."

He and the other nine contestants were whisked away, steered toward a half-circle of leather chairs that fronted Thad's podium. Darren winked as he hurried past. All 10 were shown their seats, and they spent their final torturous minutes sitting quietly, waiting for some sort of cue that taping would begin, not realizing that it already had. Eb and I settled into seats in the second row. Finally, the theater lights fell dark, and others over the stage brightened, drawing a sharp, white circle around Thad. Without further notice, he began.

"Hello America, and welcome to 'Who's Who?'," he started, mustering as serious a look as he could, "the only reality TV show that's truly real."

Thad shifted his pose and strolled at a leisurely pace toward a camera at the rear of the stage. Every step was taken with precision.

"How is it different? In countless ways, and tonight, and over the course of the next few months, you'll find out exactly how. For one, these 10 men have virtually no idea what's in store for them. They've signed on despite knowing only a few of the rules. They know only that a two-hundred and fifty thousand dollar grand prize awaits the last man standing. Not to mention a potentially lifelong relationship with a lovely young woman, but more on that in a while."

Thad paused, letting the excitement build. Three cameramen squirmed on the floor in front of the 10 men, pointing their cameras up to capture close-ups of the nervous faces that would be seen by millions of people. Darren, like most of the others, wore a pained grin. One guy bit his lip. Another shook his head as if reconsidering.

"Gentlemen," Thad continued, turning his stroll toward the contestants. "Are you ready to learn more about 'Who's Who?'?"

The group nodded in unison. Thad's talent for dragging out the drama was finely honed.

"OK, but before we delve into the details of the show, let's first let America meet these 10 gentlemen, shall we?"

It was clearly a line that would cue editors to plug in individual interviews later. In the theater, the guys took turns saying their name and hometown; a couple even tossed in an occupation. None of it would ever be aired. Instead, private interviews with each would fill the intro space. When they finished, Thad returned to the camera, no doubt to follow a beer commercial.

"OK America, we've tortured these 10 guys enough, wouldn't you say? Let's get on with it."

More smiles. More lip biting.

"You've met these 10 contestants. Now, how about a word or two on the 11th."

Necks cocked and eyes searched.

"Unfortunately, a word or two is about all I can give tonight," Thad continued with a smug grin. "I won't say her name. I won't show what she looks like. All I will say is that she's living here, in Chicago. Somewhere in the Windy City is the woman these 10 guys will spend the coming weeks and months trying to find."

Thad paused, before adding with emphasis.

"Whoever finds her will be a quarter of a million dollars richer."

Thad stopped, leaving the cast members with stupefied looks on their faces, all of which was soaked up by the cameras. It was working just as Stuart had said. Thad's pause stretched ridiculously long as the guys stared open-mouthed at one another, some laughing, and some looking perturbed. After a pause that milked every ounce of drama from the moment, Thad finally continued.

"You're probably already thinking that this show is different from the rest, and you're right. But there's more."

From 30 feet away, Darren's eyes met mine. I couldn't tell if he was amused or angry.

"The woman we've chosen has no idea she's been chosen. In time we'll let her in on our secret, but until then, only we know who she is, and we'll be secretly filming her over the next several weeks."

At this news, the theater fell into a hushed silence. Most of the guys stared at Thad puzzled. Eb looked at me with the same expression. We aren't exactly reality TV experts, but this was different from anything we'd heard about. Sidney, for one, is a big reality TV fan, and she never described anything like this.

"Now obviously, Chicago is a big city," Thad said, returning to a serious tone. "Pretty tough to find one girl in a city of millions. Fortunately, we're here to help. Throughout the process, and beginning today, we'll pass along clues that will help locate this mystery woman. Each of you will then do whatever you can to piece together the clues and ultimately find her. Just bear in mind that hidden cameras may or may not be trained on you at any time, 24/7."

Thad paused again to let the contestants absorb the details.

"Each of you has been assigned living quarters. When we're done here today, you will go to your homes. Your first clue is waiting for you there. Also awaiting you are instructions for our first Bonus Challenge, which gives each of you a chance to win an additional clue that no other contestant will have. And trust me, gentlemen, every scrap of information you can uncover, every iota of intel that steers you toward your ultimate goal, should be coveted. Because the closer you get to finding it, to finding her, the closer you get to becoming our champion. Nine of you will return home to rejoin the lives you left behind, while one of you will take home two-hundred and fifty-thousand dollars."

Thad let this sobering fact take root. Until then, the cast members hadn't bothered to remember that in a relatively short time they could be back on a plane, bound to return to a life of anonymity. Many, if not all, of these guys had hoped for only two things from their appearance on "Who's Who?" - fame and money. Three things, if you count the girl. The thought of such an unceremonious conclusion left a few of them pale.

"So gentlemen, that is your mission," Thad said as he started a slow stroll in front of the chairs on stage, sliding one hand in a pocket. "When it's over, someone will finally find this mystery woman. Someone will win a quarter of a million dollars. There are two million women in Chicago, gentlemen, and we have nearly a thousand cameras working throughout the city."

Thad paused again, rested an elbow on the edge of podium, and sent a majestic stare into the camera lens.

"Wherever you go, whoever you talk to, everywhere you look, be sure to ask yourself - Who's who?"

~

Darren plopped down hard on the padded bench across from me and reached for his bottle.

"What'd she think?" Eb asked before devouring a nacho chip that dripped cheese and bacon.

"My mom wasn't home, so I called my sister. She said it sounds crazy."

Darren swallowed deep into his beer and thought.

"It is, too, isn't it?" he said. "It's frickin' crazy."

After leaving the theater, Eb and I followed Darren to his apartment. His 10th floor balcony overlooks the Chicago River and the city that stands above it. We found his first clue there, just as Thad had said, although it wasn't much of clue really. On an index card, printed in Old English-style letters, were the words:

Clue No. 1
Gems of turquoise scatter like glowing millipedes
across a marble floor on which she walks.

Darren looked at it quietly for a minute, his forehead scrunching into a knot between his eyes.

"No idea," he said, flipping the card across the coffee table. "You guys?"

Eb read it to himself, then repeated it out loud.

"Do you know Chicago at all?" I asked Darren. "Maybe it's referring to a certain building, one with marble floors?"

Darren shrugged.

"You know, this is the first clue, it's not like we're going to solve the whole puzzle tonight," Eb said. "This has to be almost impossible, by design. Probably doesn't mean shit."

He held the card up against the light, as if its true message might be hidden in a watermark behind the huge question mark, which had become the show's logo. That's when Darren spotted a line of fine print-sized type near the corner of the back of the card.

"Hey guys, look at that," he said, reaching for the card. "There's something typed on there."

Darren pulled the card close to his face and read in a whisper.

"ENIN GUA A ETAG LIM SUSREV SBUC"

Eb was listening intently as Darren sounded out the line of gibberish. By the time Darren slowly pronounced "Sibuck," Eb wore a disgusted look on his face.

"What the hell does that mean?" he said. "Enin Gooah? Darren, read it again."

Darren stood and began pacing as he repeated the line. When he finished, he shared a blank look with the two of us before dropping the card on the table.

"Enin Gooah," Eb repeated, grabbing the card and holding it again to the light. "Ay Etag-"

Eb paused and a wide grin cut across his face.

"I got it," he said.

Darren stopped pacing, looking stunned and skeptical all at once.

"Check it out, when you hold it up and read it from the other side," Eb said. "The letters are backwards, but it's pretty obvious. 'Cubs versus Mil. Gate A. Aug. Nine.'"

Eb tossed the card to the tabletop and leaned back, gloating a bit for having decoded the clue. Darren held the card to the light to verify, then flipped it on the table for me to read.

"Unbelievable," Darren said, double- and triple-checking Eb's work. "I guess I'm going to the Cubs' game tomorrow. You guys are coming too, aren't you?"

"We're following you," Eb said. "Wherever you go, we go."

Darren looked at the card again and started to laugh, then looked at Eb and me and shrugged.

"In that case, you guys feel like following me down to the bar? I guess our work is done tonight."

Twenty minutes later we were eating nachos, drinking beer and talking about the show. Darren didn't seem to mind that I snapped pictures every now and then.

"I think my sister thinks this is a mistake, me being on the show," Darren said. "She thinks it's a waste of time."

He lifted a nacho chip to his mouth and crunched hard, not bothering to chew and swallow before continuing his thought.

"But Eb's right about this first clue," he said as a slice of black olive fell to the table. "Doesn't make sense on purpose. It probably won't make sense until later."

Eb and I agreed.

"Hell, anything is possible," Darren continued. "Dan might be right, it might have something to do with a certain building, a place with a marble floor. Maybe there's turquoise in the tile work. Maybe she lives there."

"Or works there," Eb said.

I considered all of this over the noise of Darren and Eb eating tortilla chips.

"Maybe it's a museum," Darren said, still crunching.

"Or a library," Eb added.

Our aimless guessing dragged on for an hour before the suggestions finally ran dry. During a lull in the conversation, I mentioned something we hadn't talked about yet. I guess we were sidetracked by the whole business of figuring out that clue.

"Guys, see that girl standing at the end of the bar?" I said. "Wouldn't it be weird if that's her? It could be her, right?"

As the three of us sat quietly considering the thought, I realized how many women were in the bar. I glanced out the window and noticed women walking along the sidewalks. I imagined how many others were in restaurants and stores, office buildings and homes. I flashed back to our view of the skyline when Eb and I arrived in Chicago, and suddenly Darren's mission, as Thad had referred to it, took on a larger scope.

"You know what else?" Eb said. "See that guy in the hat, over by the Walter Payton poster? He could be filming all of this. Twenty-four, seven, right?"

We scanned the room slowly, on the lookout for anybody suspicious-looking enough to be packing a hidden camera. Eventually our eyes met again over the tray of nachos. Darren shook his head as he reached for another chip.

Two tables away, a round, sweaty guy in a suit coat that was too small was standing over a table holding a video camera, filming what appeared to be a small graduation party. It probably was a small graduation party. But we questioned whether it was a small graduation party. To test it, we convinced Darren to walk a slow lap around the room while Eb and I watched to see if the fat guy with the video camera followed him. The guy never steered his lens away from his party's guest of honor, a homely girl with a pink dress, a mess of brown hair and enormous teeth. She seemed to be having a good time. The fat guy didn't appear to be the least bit interested in Darren, Eb or me.

"Nothing," Eb reported when Darren returned to our table and plopped down hard again.

For a second, the three of us felt a bit foolish. It didn't last.

"What about those two guys," Darren suggested casually, rolling his eyes over his shoulder toward two guys leaning against a wall. They were watching a White Sox game on a TV mounted high on the wall. One was wearing a baseball cap. The other wore a pair of thick-framed glasses and had what looked like a camera case slung over his shoulder.

"I'll keep an eye on them," Eb said. "It is kind of strange to be carrying that case around."

For the next half hour, we talked quietly over our nachos, as if somebody was not only watching us, but listening too. We were watchful of every move Darren made, and paid close attention to the two guys against the wall, on guard for them to do anything that didn't make sense.

It's a funny thing about cameras. The minute somebody thinks a camera is aimed at them – even if one isn't – everything from that point becomes unnatural. I see it all the time, going back to that ground-breaking for Rodgers Hall. The university administrators who were there for the occasion were joking and laughing as we got the shot set up. But the minute I took the lens cap off, their faces changed. They turned serious, as if afraid to cast the wrong image in the *Telegram*. Little kids are the worst. Once a kid sees your camera aimed at him, his whole demeanor changes. He might make a goofy face. Or pose. Or pretend not to notice you and then not do anything, which isn't close to normal. When it comes to having their picture taken, people are terrible. Once they notice your camera, it's impossible to get something real.

The minute Darren was reminded that a camera might be aimed at him, he changed. He was a little less outspoken, almost nervous. Definitely preoccupied. However you want to describe it, he wasn't the same. Suddenly it wasn't as real anymore. Eb and I weren't helping by pointing out the possible hidden cameras around the bar.

"Hey Darren, I have an idea," Eb said, still speaking in a low voice. "Get up and leave. I'll take care of the tab."

Darren stared across the table confused.

"Seriously, leave. Dan and I will meet you at that Irish bar down the street in a little bit. We'll keep an eye on the door to see if anybody follows you out."

Darren hesitated for just a second, but eventually agreed. In an overly casual manner, he stood up, stretched his arms and announced that he would see us tomorrow. What an actor. Looking back, the whole exercise was ridiculous.

Eb and I watched Darren as he left the bar, watched him through the plate-glass window until he was out of sight, and kept a vigilant watch over the room to see if anybody followed. The guys leaning against the wall were deep into the Sox game. The camera case was nowhere to be seen. The guy with the ugly niece was in a chair shoveling a cubic yard of cake into his mouth. Anybody else who had previously roused suspicion was carrying on with bar-type behavior that Eb and I deemed normal.

After what seemed a fair amount of time to do proper surveillance, Eb flagged our waitress for the tab. And then we left.

10

*With Darren
Meet at Wrigley
11:30*

The message was wordy, at least by Eb's standards. He typically spends as few syllables as possible before finding a way to fasten a note to my head. This particular one, given the limited resources in the hotel room, was scribbled on the back of a room-service menu and slipped into the collar of my t-shirt. I woke to the corner of the page poking my chin. My head was on fire.

After meeting up at the Irish pub, the three of us spent the evening bouncing from one bar to another. A thorough dissection of "Who's Who?" dominated the early part of the evening, but as the night spiraled, the TV show eventually drifted from our focus. We wound up at a bar with some girls from Milwaukee, watching a guy play folk music on an acoustic guitar. By 2:30 I'd had enough and staggered a few blocks to our hotel. Eb and Darren were still going strong.

On the walk back, I kidded myself into thinking I could fight off sleep long enough to work on my poem. I wound up on a large sill in the hotel room, leaning against the window, enjoying our 20th-floor view of the city and hoping a poem would write itself. It didn't. I fell asleep with my head against the glass, and probably would have stayed there all night had Eb not crashed in at 4:30 and stumbled over a coffee table. He landed hard on the floor, cracking his shoulder on a dresser corner on the way down. I woke to him muttering and swearing. Eb laid there for a minute before struggling to his feet and staggering into the adjoining room. The last I heard from him he was giggling, "Wait until you hear what happened." When he didn't come back, I looked in to find him sprawled out on the bed.

Five hours later the menu was jabbing my jawbone and Eb was gone. A quick shower, a crisp walk to the train station, and 20 minutes on a train pressed against a woman in desperate need of a bar of soap was more than enough to jar me awake. I was hustling toward Wrigley Field looking for Gate A when Darren spotted me from his seat on a bar patio.

"Hey camera boy, what's the hurry?"

He was munching on a celery stalk, dipping it reluctantly into a Bloody Mary.

"Hey Darren, how are you feeling? You with Eb?"

"Bathroom," he said, motioning over his shoulder. "I don't think the drink landed too well."

Two half-full glasses sat sweating on the table.

"These aren't good," he said, nudging his drink further away from his chair. "Drink up if you want."

I passed.

Eb bounded around the corner and squeezed through a pack of Cubs fans who cluttered the patio doorway. His Tigers t-shirt didn't seem to offend anybody.

"Hey D, you get my note?"

He laughed hysterically before breaking into a descriptive tale for Darren, recalling no fewer than six different ways he's managed to attach a note to my sleeping body. The electrical tape on the brow was a good one, but I doubt he'll ever top the time he used a dry-erase marker and wrote "Eating" in reverse letters across my forehead. Luckily I spotted that message in the bathroom mirror before I left the house. The whole custom seemed to fascinate Darren.

"You guys must go way back, huh?" he said during a pause in his laughter. "Were you friends growing up or something?"

It usually seems like it. Sometimes it's hard to remember being at GLU before I knew Eb.

"No, we met sophomore year," I said. Eb was attempting another drink of Bloody Mary. "I'm from the Thumb; Eb's from the East Coast."

Darren seemed satisfied with that thorough recap. I think his head hurt too badly to request and absorb more details. Eb pushed his glass away, surrendering to any thoughts of forcing down the drink. We were anxious to get to the stadium.

Eb and I settled into seats about 20 rows behind third base as the Cubs trotted off the field to end the top of the first inning. We weren't watching the game. We were looking for any sign of Darren.

"This is the right section, isn't it?" Eb asked, craning his neck while balancing a tray of nachos on his lap with one hand and holding a full beer with the other.

Section 131. We were in the right place. Better than 40,000 Chicago fans were packed into Wrigley Field, hopped up from the start. When the Cubs' leadoff hitter stepped to the plate, it was nearly impossible to see through the sea of bodies around us. Surrounded by standing Cubs fans, Eb wiped a glob of cheese from his chin, looked at me with his beer glass raised, and said, "Here's to Shipler, and to the expense report that is going to give him a heart attack." We laughed and tapped our plastic glasses.

"You guys need some peanuts with those?"

Darren was standing on the steps wearing a royal blue vest with wide apron pockets at the hips and two enormous white question marks on the front and back. None of the Cubs fans knew what it meant, but they weren't supposed to.

"What the hell are you doing?" Eb asked.

"Selling peanuts. Turns out, that's the challenge. I'm not here to watch the game, I'm here to work it."

"I like the vest," Eb said. "Can you hook me up with one of those?"

Darren grinned.

"Eb, it's funny you should ask. At the end of the inning, meet me up in the concourse."

With that, Darren held a bag of peanuts over his head and hollered out to the crowd around us, "PEANUTS! GET 'EM HERE! I'VE GOT PEANUTS!" as he began a slow climb down the steps toward the field.

Eb and I emptied our beers as the inning played out, and hurried up the steps to find Darren. He was tucked into a concrete corner in the concourse. Two vests were wadded up in his hand and a box of bagged peanuts sat at his feet.

"You guys want to help?"

At first I thought he was joking.

"I'm serious," he said, and I could tell he was. "Whoever sells the most peanuts wins the challenge and gets the extra clue. You want to help? Beer's on me tonight."

Eb was already unrolling his vest and sizing it up.

"Did they say you could do that, get other people to sell for you?" I asked.

"They didn't say I couldn't," Darren said. "They just said to sell as many peanuts as possible, and to get creative. I just look at this as getting creative."

Eb was draping the vest over his head. A huge smile emerged from the neck hole. A few Cubs fans slowed to wonder about the question mark as they walked past.

"Did they tell you anything more about the show?" Eb asked, loading his vest pockets with peanuts. "Anything more about the cameras? Or what about the girl, is she here today?"

"All they said was that she's here, but I'm not sure I believe it," Darren said. "We're spread all over the stadium. Doesn't seem fair that she would be sitting in the same section where one of us is working."

Eb and I digested the information as we put the finishing touches on our uniforms.

"Who the hell knows though," Darren added. "You guys ready to go? We have Sections 131, 132 and 133, so let's split up and each take one. I'll take the middle. When you run out of peanuts, just find me and we'll come up and get more."

Eb was primed. You'd have thought they asked him to play shortstop. He volunteered to take the section closest to home plate. I started toward the section furthest down the leftfield line, hoping to snag a foul ball as a souvenir for Sidney.

As a peanut salesman, I leave plenty to be desired. I was happy to contribute to Darren's cause, but I stuck to a relatively mundane sales pitch, yelling "PEANUTS!"

every half-minute while strolling up and down the steps. Darren's approach was a bit more flamboyant, and his sales numbers reflected it. And then there was Eb. He was a show all by himself. Whenever the stadium noise fell, I could hear him hollering, almost singing, a variety of pitches he quickly dreamed up. He lobbed bags of peanuts 30 feet away without worrying about collecting money until it was convenient. By the fourth inning, Eb became a sideshow to the game and the fans loved him. Every inning he would come up with something more outrageous than the previous. Most of the time, I wasn't able to hear him, I could only see him dancing up and down the aisles, juggling bags of peanuts, even stepping on top of the dugout before a security guard ordered him down. At one point, when the crowd quieted in between innings, I heard him yelling, "IF YOU AREN'T EATING PEANUTS, YOU MIGHT AS WELL BE ROOTING FOR THE WHITE SOX!" He wound up out-selling Darren and me combined.

It's amazing how fast a baseball game passes when you're doing something like selling peanuts. When the three of us met in the concourse in the middle of the eighth inning, Darren was in tears on the ground, and Eb was standing over him chuckling proudly.

"Did you see - ," Darren cried, pointing at Eb but struggling to finish his sentence. "Did you see what Ebner just did - ," (snort), "on the way back up here?"

Darren's giddiness was contagious and I laughed like I knew the story.

"That last trip up the steps - ," Darren's face was bright red, "he held the peanuts over his head -"

Darren fended off bursts of laughter before he stood to finish the story with an imitation.

"He walked up the steps - ," snort, "and hollered over and over - ," snort, "'LAST CHANCE TO EAT MY NUTS!' It was the funniest damn thing I've ever seen."

Reliving the episode sent Darren back into an eye-watering seizure, and he grabbed a railing to keep from collapsing again to the concrete.

"So journalism, huh?" he paused to suck the barbecue sauce from his hands one finger at a time. In the two days that I spent with Darren, his table manners were without question his most irritating quality. "When are you done?"

"Wednesday. One final and that's it," I said.

"For good? You're graduating? Man, that's got to be an awesome feeling."

I agreed.

"How about you, you almost finished?"

"I was on pace to graduate in the spring," Darren said. "Until this came up."

Darren and I fell silent. Our idle chatter was no match for what really had our attention. Between comments, we quietly alternated glances between the TV above the bar showing ESPN and two men in Cubs hats sitting near the jukebox. Eb suspected them as cameramen. We had planned on disregarding the potential for hidden cameras, but that strategy was erased quickly with Eb's suspicions. Every now and then Darren's eyes would return to mine, and he'd shrug before resuming his attempt to devour a mound of chicken wings piled in a basket large enough to be holding laundry.

The contest was called The Wing Fling, and Darren jumped at the challenge the second Eb assured him there was no chance in hell of finishing the entire serving. Anyone who could stomach enough poultry was awarded dinner on the house, their picture on the wall, and a t-shirt that read, 'Fling Me A Wing...I Ate The Whole Damn Thing." The fact that Darren attempted it in full view of what he suspected were hidden TV cameras seemed strange, but I didn't bring it up. I don't think any of us actually believed there were hidden cameras.

"How did all this happen? How did you get on 'Who's Who?' in the first place?"

"Actually, it wasn't even my idea," he said. "One of my roommates heard about it and thought it would be funny to send my name in. One day, some guy calls about the audition. Two weeks later I drove down to Detroit. The whole thing was crazy. I really didn't want to do it because of school and everything, but when else am I going to get the chance to win this kind of money?"

Eb returned from the bathroom, trying to hide suspicious glances as he walked past the guys in the Cubs hats. He motioned toward the stack of chicken bones as he lowered into his seat.

"A lot left. I don't think you're gonna make it."

Darren nodded confidently, gnawed the meat from a wing to further his point, and then peeked toward the jukebox.

"Anything interesting over there?"

Eb shook his head and looked innocently to the opposite side of the bar. What masterful deception. Our concern was that if a hidden camera was aimed at us, it would have to be equipped with some sort of microphone that could pick up audio from a distance. Why we didn't want potential cameramen to know we had spotted them, I'm not sure. Looking back on it, it seems the best way to counter a hidden cameraman would be to let him know that he isn't hidden.

Maybe it was because he was preoccupied with hidden cameras that Darren, better than two hours after taking his first bite, ate his way through the entire basket of wings. Or maybe it was because he eats like a hog. A small crowd of waitresses gathered around the table to watch as Darren slowed the last wing into his mouth. I was standing next to Eb, who hovered over Darren's shoulder emceeing the event. Darren's face was weary, his eyes sagging with the weight of about 150 chicken wings. The wait staff erupted into song when the final bit of meat was chewed and swallowed. A stream of people in the bar made a point to pass our table to offer congratulations and disbelief. Darren slouched heavy in his chair and appeared to be on the verge of vomiting. At some point during the celebration, the guys wearing the Cubs hats slipped out without any of us noticing.

11

We pulled from the hotel parking garage at about 3 o'clock on Sunday afternoon. By 3:15, Eb had the passenger seat fully reclined and was sound asleep. Four straight nights of binging had taken a toll.

Eb and I met Darren earlier that afternoon at a restaurant near his apartment, sort of a farewell meal that would give Eb one last chance to gather information for the stories he was writing. I brought my camera, but I didn't even take it out of its case. I had everything I needed. We passed around a copy of the *Sun-Times*, which included a small blurb about a new reality TV show that had begun filming in Chicago. The article was extremely vague, probably exactly what Stuart wanted.

Lunch was quiet, tamed by lingering effects of an evening that bounced throughout downtown Chicago, landed for late-night beers at Darren's apartment, and faded gently with a 5 a.m. cab ride to our hotel. None of us were having much luck with lunch.

Only 48 hours earlier, Eb and I didn't know Darren beyond a name that Shipler had printed and passed along. Eb had talked only briefly with him on the phone. Essentially, Darren Morrell was a complete stranger. Maybe it was because we had spent two straight days experiencing something as unknown as reality TV. Maybe it was because we were three guys who, at least for the weekend, were lifted from our homes in northern Michigan and dropped in an enormous city like Chicago. Whatever it was, when Eb and I left the restaurant it was surprisingly emotional. I don't mean we were hugging and crying or anything, but saying goodbye to Darren felt like saying goodbye to a longtime friend.

We all shook hands and agreed to stay in touch. Darren promised to keep us informed of what was happening on the show, and Eb and I urged him to call if he needed help with any other clues. And then we left. It's hard to describe, but it felt strange leaving him to continue on without us. The last I saw him, through a large window at the front of the restaurant, Darren was finishing his coffee and looking again at the article in the *Sun-Times*. He was sitting by himself, but what really struck me was how alone he looked.

The heavy traffic getting out of the city made me long for Wanishing. We were expecting to be back by sunset, and I spent the miles listening to Eb snore and listing in my head everything I had to do when we got back to town. Since Shipler was going to want images from our trip as early as possible the next morning, I was leaning toward putting in some late-night darkroom time when we got back. That menu project for Ruby's had to be completed. And there was still the matter of writing a poem. I was stalled on the opening line, and I tried imagining what Sidney might do to coach something out of me.

That's what I was thinking about as we drove through Indiana. It was right around that time, as near as I could determine after reading the report in the *Daily Mirror* a few days later, sometime when we were traveling between Chicago and the Michigan state line, that Lydia Styles pulled to the curb near her home in Arizona and rubbed her eyes. Her blurred vision had returned, and worse than ever. Stan Lundwick, the *Daily Mirror* reporter who covered the story, did a remarkable job of recounting the entire episode.

The blurred vision problem had bothered Lydia previously, Lundwick reported, but she had attributed it to over-worked, tired eyes courtesy of her job as a data entry specialist. But on that day, behind the wheel of her Lexus, it got to be too much. A half-mile from her house in suburban Phoenix, Lydia pulled over. She flagged down a 70-year-old man who was walking his dog, and he pounded on the door of the nearest home to use the phone.

A blood pressure test in the back of the ambulance returned some disturbingly high numbers – 250 over 140. Further tests at a nearby hospital revealed an even scarier fact: the capillaries in Lydia's retinas were bleeding.

In Michigan, the temperature had fallen at least 10 degrees from the scorching heat of mid-summer, the first sign of the coming fall. It was comfortable in the Cherokee, and Eb's nap continued uninterrupted. I was both anxious to get home and enjoying the hours of quiet as we sped up the freeway toward Saugatuck.

The sun continued its long, slow fall toward Lake Michigan, blasting me from the west as I turned north onto the M-37. When we passed the Hilltop Tavern I thought about Mac and Jimmer, and wondered what they might do to fill their time on a lazy late-summer Sunday afternoon. I recalled something Mac had said, and I tinkered with different ways to use the words in my poem.

If my math and imagination are correct, activity around Lydia Styles' hospital bed was hectic at that point. Her kidneys were failing, according to that report in the *Mirror*. Dialysis appeared likely. A transplant remained a possibility. Lundwick explained in unnecessary detail how Lydia's husband was finally able to contact her twin brother.

"I told him, 'She's stable, but be prepared. We'll know more when the test results are back,'" the story quoted him as saying.

Eb's slumber continued as the setting sun left an unending shadow across our path through the Manistee National Forest. Even from a couple of hours away I could feel the comfortable familiarity of Wanishing pulling me closer. I figure it was about the time we pulled into the drive behind our house, give or take a half-hour, that Lydia's test results came back. Her condition had worsened. The possibility that she would need a transplant had become more real, and her twin brother was immediately considered the most likely suitable donor. Lundwick sure did his legwork rounding up technical information from a local doctor. He also managed to get a few minutes on the phone with Lydia's husband, and fattened the story with some meaningless fluff from a couple of Lydia's former teachers at Wanishing High. Lundwick is one of the more veteran reporters on the *Mirror* staff, and his story left nothing to question.

Kidney Failure Hospitalizes Wanishing Native in Ariz.

By Stan Lundwick
Daily Mirror Senior Writer

Lydia Styles, a 1987 graduate of Wanishing High, was hospitalized for symptoms consistent with kidney failure near her residence in Arizona Sunday afternoon.

On Monday, Styles' twin brother Darren Morrell was rushed to suburban Phoenix from his home in Chicago in preparation for a potential kidney transplant.

Morrell, also a 1987 Wanishing graduate as well as a student at Great Lakes University, is currently residing in Chicago as a cast member on the upcoming reality television series, "Who's Who?".

The story went on for 25 inches, and was accompanied by a sidebar recapping the *Mirror* report from a day earlier that described Darren's role on the show, the unofficial start of the "Who's Who?" craze in Wanishing. Our story in the *Telegram* added to it a day later.

I knew none of the Lydia Styles story when we arrived back in town. I knew only that Shipler was going to want his pictures, so I resisted the urge to collapse on the couch and instead went to campus to develop. I created contact sheets that showed dozens of pictures, and from those chose about 20 that I actually printed. I had to trash some because they violated the disclosure rules that Stuart laid out, but I was confident that Shipler had more than enough to choose from. A close-up of Darren during the taping. A wide-angle that showed him selling peanuts at Wrigley. Another close-up on his balcony. As I surveyed my work hours later, I was impressed with the collection. I stepped from the doors of Jameson Hall beneath a star-clustered black sky, into night air that delivered a chill. It was past 4 in the morning. I wanted to be home, asleep.

Sleep came quick. I cast aside thoughts of the poem that had been nagging, thoughts of the job for Orange Cat that was due the next day, and thoughts of the new job I was starting the next week at the *Daily Mirror*. Sleep came so quick I wasn't thinking about anything. Usually I need to distract myself to sleep by thinking about something. But not that night. Or morning. Whatever it was. The days and nights get jumbled sometimes. Sleep came quick and hard and lasted for most of the next day. At some point while I slept, Darren Morrell – who had just spent two days describing to Eb and me the life-altering experience of starring on a reality TV show – was leaving those prospects behind, hurrying to O'Hare Airport to possibly save his sister's life.

12

"One month to go," Jim said shaking his head as he stepped through the garage door, a fresh bottle in each hand. "Twenty-eight days, to be exact. It's going to feel like 28 weeks."

Ten minutes earlier Janine had summoned him in her standard way, by moaning his name through the bathroom window. Jim drained his bottle and hustled inside where he used his strong hands to massage her lower back and hips, trying to ease her to sleep. It was a ritual that repeated itself a half-dozen times during the evening, each time leaving me alone in the Golds' backyard to admire the life they've created for themselves. Not everybody admires it. Eb scoffs at the thought of it. Sidney calls it "sweet," though I'm not sure how badly she wants it for herself. Some days I think the Golds have it made, a quiet little paradise with jobs they enjoy and kids they love. Headquarters of their world is a comfortable, three-bedroom home in a quiet part of town, just far enough from campus to avoid any keg party casualties. Other days I wonder if either Jim or Janine ever regrets missing something. Something else. It never seems like it.

Jim's trips inside were frequent but usually quick, and every time he'd come bounding back through the garage door ready to resume where we'd left off.

"Damn tailbone is killing her," he winced, as if his own was sore. "Maybe I'm just not remembering it, but it doesn't seem like she was this bad off the first two times."

Jane and Lily were tucked quietly in their beds, every night at 9:30. Even at eight-months pregnant, Janine was a real sergeant about it. And she herself, after lugging an extra 30 pounds around all day, was worn out before the sun went down. The problem was getting her comfortable, and once that happened, Jim retreated to a little space he's claimed for himself in the backyard. His horseshoe pits are lighted for after-hours play, and he keeps a fridge nearby in the garage fully stocked. That's pretty much all he needs through the summer months, and most nights, all he wants. Jim loves his family, but on evenings like the one after Eb and I got back from Chicago, when Janine and the girls are in bed and Jim has the run of the place, he's in heaven.

With the horseshoe pit lights off, darkness was settling in over the Golds' backyard. Shadows from the stakes had stretched as far as they'd go before hiding in the Wanishing night. I lobbed a couple of errant shoes through the dark, missed the sand and then joined Jim next to the bonfire. Logs crackled in the night air as the two of us settled into a pair of padded patio chairs. Jim asked about Chicago, if we'd made it to the bar he mentioned, if we'd gotten a chance to see Soldier Field. His appetite for beer was remarkable, and after another trip to the garage he returned with a small cooler. Our voices steadily quieted, the way voices do around a fire.

"Tell you what, Danny, I was in Chicago, it would have been eight or nine years ago, not long before Janine and I got married," he said. "It's hard to believe what's happened since then. We've had two kids and have a third one on the way, we've gone through two apartments and now the house, Janine's had three different jobs, and we've had four different cars, not counting the department truck."

The light in the bathroom clicked on, cutting a line across the backyard, and Jim sighed. He'd gotten comfortable.

"Maybe it's one of the girls this time," he prayed.

A minute later the light blinked off and Jim returned his attention to the fire. He set a few more hunks of pine in the heart of the flame and the blaze lit a circle around the yard. We could have barbecued a moose. We slid our chairs back a few feet, swallowed some beer in silence and watched the heat dance beneath the logs.

"Twenty-eight days," I said. "Then the easy part."

"Shit, I'll tell you what," he grinned. "We were lucky with the first two. They started sleeping through the night after only a couple of weeks. I'm a little worried we won't get lucky three times in a row."

Jim stared at the fire, his eyes never leaving the flames, even when he drank.

"You know, it's strange Danny."

"What's that?"

"Just how things work out sometimes," Jim paused and the crickets got louder. "We had the two girls and Janine was convinced that I really wanted a boy. To tell the truth, I kind of do, but it's not a deal-breaker. Actually I think she wants one more than I do. From the moment she got pregnant, we've talked about how we're hoping for a boy. But the closer we get to the due date, the less it seems to matter."

Jim's face flickered in light from the jumping flames.

"It's just strange."

I responded by doing the only thing that seemed fitting. I raised my bottle between us, waited for him to meet me and said, "Here's to number three."

"To number three," he repeated before drinking to the bottom of another bottle. When it was gone, he dug deep into the cooler for two more and handed me one without asking.

"And to the start of a career," he said, holding a bottle between us again. "When do you start downtown?"

"Week from today. No break, I'm jumping right in."

"That's good, I'm happy for you, and I'm happy for us," he said. "Hoping you can keep shooting stuff the department's doing. We appreciate the coverage."

"I hope so too," I said. "They told me I'd be able to go out and find stories on my own. If I wind up shooting grip-and-grins and writing captions every day, I'll go crazy."

In the quiet of Jim's backyard, we talked until 3, skipping between stories of Lamaze classes and chicken-eating contests. "Who's Who?" had become a pretty hot topic around Wanishing and Jim liked having an inside track to details that nobody else knew. I told him to watch for Thad McCormick and that dimple, and how Stuart was like a little real-life cartoon character. He asked about Sidney and my final poetry class, and I asked about Jane, who is starting kindergarten this fall. He recalled his wedding day, and the day he signed the mortgage papers for the house. I told him about Orange Pile and the people at the Hilltop.

The fire had faded to ashes by the time Jim doused it with water and ice from the cooler. I wobbled as I stood, promised I'd be in touch and started a long walk home through the cool air. I barely remember walking, but Wanishing felt like it sprawled for miles that night.

༄

I stepped between two thick strands of willow leaves and found Sidney using clothes pins to hang index cards from random branches. She was facing away from me, standing on her knees, and as she reached high to pinch another branch, her white t-shirt lifted, revealing her middle back. I felt myself sweating.

"What's this?"

"Hey, there you are," she said, looking over her shoulder. "Just a writing exercise that I think will help."

Sidney had already hung at least 20 index cards of all different pastel colors. When she finished clipping the rest to the tree, she sat with her legs crossed and looked at the cards dangling over her head.

"What do you think?" she asked.

Pink and yellow and green and orange and white rectangles floated above her, waving only slightly with the movement of the tree.

"I don't know what to think, since I don't know what we're doing," I said, joining her on the ground below the cave of willow branches. "Looks cool, though."

"We've got less than one day," she beamed, rifling through her bag to find a black marker. "We've got work to do. And besides, this will be fun."

Forgetting about the index cards, Sidney proceeded to spend an hour pressing me for every detail of our trip to Chicago. She asked about the drive, the hotel room, Darren, the TV show, and every story I came back with prompted a new barrage of questions. She gushed at our chance to go to Wrigley, stared in amazement as I described the taping at the Clark Theater, and gasped as I recounted our near head-on collision. She seemed almost disappointed that she didn't have the chance to see Stuart up-close. I love how Sidney can be fascinated by the most trivial things.

"What an amazing experience," she said. "I was thinking about it while you were gone, it might actually end up being a better opportunity for you and Eb than it is for Darren."

The comment surprised me.

"I mean, if he doesn't win, then what?" she explained. "He probably just comes back to school and picks up where he left off, right? You and Eb are going to have something to show for it no matter what."

I hadn't thought of it that way. Sidney has a real knack for spinning something and looking at it from an angle that would never occur to me.

"Of course, if he wins it's a different story," she laughed, which returned us to the backstage experience at the theater. She wanted to know everything, which is exactly what I told her. I didn't worry about the release forms. It was Sidney; I could tell her anything.

"So, during all the fun, I doubt you managed to get any work done on your poem," she said, feigning a smug smile.

"Nope."

"I figured, that's what these are for," she said, motioning again to the cards that fluttered overhead. "You ready?"

Sidney went on to describe a somewhat elaborate exercise designed to help encourage the type of word play that might inspire a poem. We took turns pulling a card from a branch and writing a word on it before returning it to its place in the tree. When the cards were all used, Sidney grabbed another handful of clothes pins and another stack of cards from her bag, and we continued on. When we were done, we laid beneath a cloud of dangling index cards, the colors twinkling against the soft green of the tree leaves. I'm not sure what the exercise accomplished to help me write my final poem. In fact, I'm not sure it helped me at all. But I didn't care.

13

I don't know why I was worried, I honestly don't. Every poem I wrote for Carroll's class was a piece of garbage, but knowing the level of talent that surrounded me should have provided a certain level of comfort. Plus, like Eb had told me, "The best part about poetry class is that there are no wrong answers. Just bad answers."

I stopped at The Snack Shack on my way to class to give my poem a final polishing. Re-reading it didn't help my confidence. When I finally stepped into Carroll's room I felt like I was going to throw up.

Carroll was seated on the front edge of his desk, ready to mediate the final readings. The chairs were full save for one, which I expected, but instead of landing a spot next to Sidney I was forced to slide in between Arnold Kelch and Aimee Greer. Sidney glanced up and waved hello from across the half-circle. After a few brief words and comments on how he would be surmising our final grades, Carroll circled behind his desk and began his random calling of people to read. I prayed I wasn't first.

"Mr. Kelch, why don't you get us started?" Carroll said as he reclined back in his seat and hoisted his cowboy boots to the edge of the desk.

Arnold's lungs, already struggling in the summer humidity, were further challenged by a near-deadly case of nerves. He was breathing like a horse and I thought for a second he might pass out. Sidney and I shared a quiet laugh across the room as Arnold sped through a real gem, something about his dog. When he was done, he sat and looked first at Carroll and then at his desk, his cheeks a pulsing red that gleamed with sweat. I expected him to wet himself. Carroll didn't say anything, just peered through his bifocals to see if anybody was going to comment voluntarily. After a moment of silence, he thanked Arnold and offered a brief courtesy analysis that somehow ignited about five minutes of classroom discussion. Arnold, who barely looked up from his notebook as the class tossed around various thoughts on his poem, sagged with relief the moment Carroll turned everybody's attention to the next victim.

Pam Kinney is a 43-year-old Wanishing native, as out of place on campus as a pro-war rally. She wears polyester slacks that are snug in all the wrong places, speaks endlessly of her two children, who by little coincidence went away to college, and writes poetry that hurts to hear. Her standard work typically deals with topics like child rearing or housework. Earlier in the summer she treated the class to "Those Dirty Dishes," 16 forgettable lines that, for some reason, Carroll elected to read aloud. I think he quietly shared the humor in it with the rest of us.

Pam lifted herself from the chair wearing the same blank smile she always does, eager to share her work with the class one last time. It was painful. The talent she lacks in writing poetry is matched by an inability to read aloud, and for a torturous one minute and 47 seconds, all of which I counted closely on the clock above the blackboard, Pam stumbled through an epic piece of crap that centered on the rigors of making the perfect dinner. That damn smile, it was like she was constipated, sliced across her face as she read the final line, and she scanned the room eager for feedback. All she got were a few warmed over comments about how that was her best poem yet.

Suddenly I wanted to go next. I was just about to throw my hand in the air to volunteer when Carroll called on Aimee. Sidney saw it and grinned. Aimee hurried through a quick but decent little poem about her dead grandma. The discussion that followed lasted more than the standard 30 seconds, with people trading thoughts on Aimee's usage of certain words and her amazing ability to rhyme lines without making it too obvious. I was watching Sidney, who was sitting back and absorbing a small debate regarding Aimee's usage of the phrase "after life" when she raised her hand and offered that Aimee's poem, more important than anything, was heartfelt and must have been difficult to write. Aimee actually appeared on the verge of tears.

The conversation raged for 10 minutes, with Carroll occasionally dropping in seemingly unrelated anecdotes. Through it all, I felt my name inching its way up the list. Those prize works from Kelch and Pam helped ease my nerves a little, but I sure didn't want to follow anything decent. Sidney, on the other hand, was as calm as ever. Carroll finally managed to put an end to the discussion with a vague comment that left everybody confused, and then continued on.

"Sidney, why don't we hear from you next?"

She didn't look the least bit fazed. Sidney seldom does. She stood up casually, brushed the hair from the rim of her glasses and said through her soft smile, "This is called 'Forever Since An Apple.'"

She cleared her throat quietly and without referring to the paper in her hand, read.

"Gather stones and see the way your life's been spent.
Trip the mockingbird and lose its luscious scent.
Collecting lilacs on a most delicious day.
But forever since an apple came my way."

She sat without looking at all embarrassed. She didn't look arrogant, just happy. I think she really liked what she had written. Carroll peered through his glasses wearing an expression that showed sudden and rare interest.

"What does Sidney mean when she says these lines?" he asked, rising to his feet.

Nearly everyone just stared at him. A few studied their desks. Kelch was using his pen to dig a clump of dirt from the treads of his shoes. I glanced at Sidney, who was eager for response. And then, in an unprecedented move, Carroll began dissecting the four lines. Word by word he delved into the poem, and in another stunning turn, he called for opinion.

"Daniel, what did you think?"

Suddenly I had to go to the bathroom. I fidgeted in my seat and tried to replay the four lines in my head. *Trip the mockingbird? A delicious day?* I remembered portions from our time under the willow tree, but had no interpretation to offer. I searched for anything relevant to say.

"Uh, I'm not sure what this poem's intentions were," I managed, trying to come up with something abstract enough that people might mistake it for analysis. Sidney giggled quietly.

"I'm not trying to dodge the question, I just really don't know. But I will say this. I like the way it sounded."

Without request, others began chiming in, offering an opinion of the meaning of this phrase, an interpretation of that word. Sidney and I glanced around the room, listening to what the others were saying, but sharing our own quiet conversation whenever our eyes met in the middle. I shrugged, as if asking, "What was I supposed to say?" She laughed to herself before joining the discussion, shedding light on what her poem meant. I was oblivious. I watched her as the chattering voices surrounded me. I watched her and thought about our next walk to the Sands, looking forward to whatever slice of time we could spend together. I watched her, and for at least a few minutes forgot all about my turn to read coming up.

It eventually came, last on the list, and I endured it without injury. "Fifteen Hours Later" was well-received, all things considered. After a few minutes of irrelevant commentary, Carroll closed the summer semester with a 20-minute-long verbal wandering that went nowhere and said nothing. We were free to go. As I stepped one last time from a flight of stairs into the courtyard surrounding Briar Hall, Sidney looked at me and said, "Congratulations! You're done!"

I thanked her and promised to return the sentiment a year later. We walked north across campus, past the willow tree, through occasional pockets of students celebrating their final classroom visit. I felt relieved, partly because the poem was behind me, partly because I had graduated.

"Big plans for tonight?" Sidney asked as we strolled. "Celebrating with Eb probably?"

"Maybe. Not sure. How about you, anything planned?"

Sidney shook her head. "Kyle's practicing. They're getting ready for the CD release party next week, so I haven't seen much of him lately."

A group of students gathered in the plaza. Sidney and I walked through the loud music not bothering to battle the volume with conversation. As the party faded behind us, so did Sidney's mention of Kyle.

"So tell me, what was your apple poem all about?"

Sidney grinned, I'm sure recalling my insightful comments in class.

"Actually that line came from a different poem I was writing earlier this summer," she said. "I never finished it, but I always liked the line."

She really did too, I could tell.

"So what's it mean? What's the poem about?"

At the north edge of campus across from the Snack Shack, Sidney stopped and leaned against a wooden fence post. She looked like a picture from a GLU brochure.

"I'm not telling," she said, still smiling. "I'll show you instead. You busy tomorrow?"

"Nope, free until Monday, I'm all yours," I said, immediately regretting my choice of words.

"Great. Meet me at Freedom Park. About noon."

With that, we went our separate ways, and I hurried toward home, anxious to join Eb in reading the *Telegram* and our front-page spread.

14

Apostrophe was stretched out in the shade of the metal bench, every inch of him pressed against the porch floor except for those three inches of tail. An empty tin sat in front of his face. Eb must have heard me bounding up the wooden steps because by the time I reached the door he was calling out highlights from the *Telegram*.

"Full front page, D," he called. "A jump page on 7, and an entire spread on 8 and 9!"

The Brumler feature a week earlier had nothing on this.

"Have you seen it yet?" he gushed as I rounded into the kitchen, where three copies of the paper laid spread across the table. "Check this out!"

Shipler and the gang had sure gotten some mileage out of our weekend trip. A huge close-up of Darren dominated the front cover, surrounded by a collage of images from the weekend, the first few paragraphs of Eb's lead article and a 100-point headline that read, "RISING

STAR." Much like a week earlier, bylines for both Eb and me were called out in large, bold type.

Eb's story jumped inside, where it wrapped around a picture of Darren in the makeup chair. A column that Eb wrote, in which he basically explained why we were restricted from publishing certain details about the show, ran the length of the page. Another seven of my photos were shown as a gallery to fill the center spread, along with a couple of small sidebars that Eb wrote. I have to admit, it was an impressive package.

"Check this out," Eb said, pointing to a picture of the Chicago skyline, its buildings cut out and stretched across the bottom edge of the center spread.

"How are the stories?" I asked. "Did they mess with them?"

"No, not too much. Couple of minor edits here and there, but nothing bad."

Eb proceeded to run his finger down the entire lead story, stopping occasionally to describe any changes that were made. There were only a couple that seemed to bother him. As he started the same exercise with his column, the phone pulled him away, leaving me to scan the articles on my own. I hadn't read any of it ahead of time. It was by far the best work Eb had done for the *Telegram*.

"This is Ebner, who's calling?" he said, back at the table appraising the coverage.

"Stuart who? Oh, Stuart, yeah, how's it going? Dan and I are reading the paper now. Looks great."

He quieted, listening with mild interest.

"Yeah, I heard, kidney failure. Is she OK?"

Eb looked at me and shrugged.

"Oh, no shit, a transplant?" he said. "How's Darren? I called him last night but he didn't answer."

Eb stopped reading, sat back in his chair and gave his full attention to the phone.

"He had to leave?"

I stopped reading too.

"When is he going to be back?"

Eb's head rolled back and an ache spread across his face.

"For good? You mean leaving, as in leaving the show? Holy shit."

Eb looked at me and shook his head.

"This is unbelievable. Do you know how I can get ahold of him?"

Eb scribbled a phone number over a photo in the newspaper then froze.

"Me? What are you talking about?"

A look that was all at once curious and excited and skeptical spread across Eb's face as he stood and began pacing the kitchen floor.

"Can you do that? You already started filming."

Eb was circling between the living room and kitchen, a frenzy in his voice. I had forgotten about the newspapers on the table and was trying to pry information out of him.

"Darren had to leave the show," he whispered, cupping the mouthpiece of the phone. "They want me to take his place."

From there, Eb unleashed an assault of questions, each of which Stuart was quick to answer. I was wondering right along with him. How long would he be gone? When did he need to be there? As Eb took his pacing to the porch where he could light a cigarette, I lowered back into my chair at the kitchen table, shaken by a blend of excitement and disappointment that I can't describe.

I looked again at the newspapers strewn in front of me. Four full pages of coverage. Four full pages of coverage that included 15 photos, three articles and two sidebars. Shipler devoted more than a quarter of the summer's final edition of the *Campus Telegram* to a feature on GLU student Darren Morrell and his upcoming spot as a cast member on a reality TV show. Eb and I drove five hours to Chicago, spent two days with Darren, and produced a mountain of content.

Four full pages of coverage. Overnight, our lead story was reduced to fiction. Not one bit of it was true.

The rest of the afternoon and evening was a torrent of hysteria and uncertainty. Eb and I had been planning a celebration in honor of my finishing college and of our story being published. The phone call from Stuart put a new spin on the celebration. Instead of doing the bar circuit, we filled our refrigerator and raced through the apartment rounding up Eb's stuff and hauling it down to the Cherokee. Through it all, Eb replayed his conversation with Stuart. By the end of the evening he began at least 100 sentences with "Stuart said."

"Stuart said they needed to move fast," Eb explained as he transferred clothes from his dresser drawers to two over-sized duffle bags. "He said they have some alternates on standby, but he convinced the producers that it would make more sense to get me. I guess I show up in some of the footage. At Wrigley, at the bar when Darren was eating those chicken wings."

Both seemed like memories from weeks, even months ago.

"So we were right, huh?" I asked. "Those guys in Cubs hats had hidden cameras?"

Eb shrugged.

"Stuart said they would just have to do some creative editing to fix what they filmed at the theater. He said people will never even notice there was a change."

"Unless somebody read today's *Telegram*," I said.

"I asked him about that. Stuart said it wouldn't matter."

Eb told me whatever details he could, which weren't many. He didn't know where he would be living. Stuart said he'd take care of the arrangements. Naturally Eb was still waiting for his new phone number. Stuart said he'd take care of that too. And he didn't know how long he'd be gone. Stuart said at least a month, and more details would be available in the coming weeks.

By 9:30 we had nearly everything Eb owns crammed into his Cherokee. With the heavy lifting done, we settled onto the porch to drink beer in the cool evening air. Apostrophe was in heaven.

As the sun disappeared behind the woods to the west, we talked about Chicago, a city Eb had never stepped foot in until the previous week, but that he was now going to call home. At least for a few weeks. That's what Eb said, but I didn't believe it. From the minute I heard Eb was getting called back to take Darren's place, I never once thought that he would be home in a few weeks. Eb is not the type of guy who is going to just appear on a reality show. Eb is the type who, if he's going to be on a reality show, he's going to be the star of it. That's just the way Eb is.

15

D
Gotta run
Eb

I woke up to a candy wrapper glued to my temple with a chewed bit of bubble gum. I didn't even care. It was past 11 and I had less than an hour to get to the park to meet Sidney.

Eb and I were up past 4 in the morning, sitting at the kitchen table playing black jack for shots of beer. Eb was greased. I was too, and I stumbled toward the hallway and my room. Eb was staring at the kitchen table top.

"Hey D, do something," he mumbled, stopping me as I passed through the doorway into the hall.

I leaned my forehead against the wall, not really trying to respond and not sure how I would anyway.

"You know. You gotta do something."

I pretended that I didn't know what he was talking about and continued to my room. The last thing I remember is Eb calling down the hallway, "D, don't do nothing. You'll regret it."

⁂

"This better be good," I said, pulling Sidney from the book she was reading.

The ground beneath the tree was dry after a full morning of sun. Hell, a full summer of sun. It hadn't rained in Wanishing in more than a month. Sidney was lying on her stomach in the shade. Her sandals sat in the grass beside her. Her faded blue jean cutoffs were frayed on her thighs, and a baggy white t-shirt highlighted her tan.

"Hey, you finally made it," she said, lifting her eyes from the pages. "I was starting to think you left me sitting here."

We spent the next hour talking about Eb getting called to appear on "Who's Who?". The sun hung like a hazy bulb at the top of the sky, and I was thankful for the shade. Just walking to Freedom Park I'd gotten sticky. As Sidney listened, a light breeze pushed strands of hair in front of her eyes, but her gaze never strayed.

"So, what is the apple poem all about?" I asked after Sidney ran out of questions about Eb.

"It's a game," she said. "My sisters and I played when we were kids. You're probably going to think it's stupid, but don't laugh."

I promised her I wouldn't.

"My mom showed us. I think she played when she was growing up. You don't keep score or anything like that. It's just something she showed us. We used to play all the time under this huge apple tree in our backyard. It was a lot bigger than this one."

I just listened.

"We lay under the tree," she said, flipping to her back and lowering her head to the grass, "and we watch for an apple to fall. If one falls, you're supposed to try and catch it."

I watched her stare up at the branches. Honestly, at first I thought she was kidding.

"That's it?" I asked, maybe too incredulously.

"Mm-hmm."

"You mean we're just supposed to lay here, stare up at the tree and wait for an apple to fall?"

"Yep," she said and laid her head back down, "and if one falls, we try to catch it."

I paused a second, just to make sure there wasn't more.

"Am I allowed to move? I mean, if I see one fall, can I dive over to try and grab it?"

"I guess," she said. "We never really made a lot of rules."

Part of me still thought she was joking, even as I cleared away a few of the apples that had already fallen. I checked her again for a smile, and when I saw she was serious I laid my head next to hers with my feet angled out the opposite way. I couldn't believe it. That was what she wanted to show me. That was the big surprise, the inspiration for her poem. I'm not sure what I was expecting, but I know it wasn't that.

We both laid there quietly, it seemed like for hours. I felt a light breeze in my hair and the grass in my fingers as I stared up into the tree. The back corner of the park was quiet. Most of the kids stay up near the fountain in the summer. The distant squeak of a swing's chain, miles away it seemed, was about all I could hear. Probably 20 minutes passed without either of us saying a word. I wasn't sure if we were allowed to talk, but finally I couldn't stand it anymore.

"Hey Sid?" I said, almost whispering.

"Yeah?"

"Is this what you were doing when I saw you down here earlier this summer?"

For a second I felt guilty, as if I had interrupted her doing something important.

"No, I just came to read," she said. "June's too early anyway. The apples weren't ready to fall then."

It was obvious Sidney didn't want to talk, but after a few more minutes I couldn't resist.

"Hey Sid?"

"Yeah?" she whispered.

"Do you come down here and play this a lot?" I asked, rolling to my side to face her.

In a nearby tree, two squirrels brawled playfully.

"Not that often. The season has to be right. This isn't even that great of a time, but we might get lucky. In about a month, that's when it gets better. I just wanted to show you what my poem was about."

I could have talked forever with her about that game, that's how fascinated I was. But it was obvious Sidney just wanted to lay quietly, so I played along. I laid back and debated different strategies, wondering if there was a smart way to play it. Should I zero in on one apple and hope I picked one that fell? Should I frame as much of the tree as possible in case one fell a few branches away? And how far would I be able to lunge? And how quickly? How much time would I even have? There were a lot of factors to consider. Eb would be great at it. Eb would lay there for three minutes and have a whole strategy put together.

I lasted another five or 10 minutes before I cocked my neck to catch a glimpse of Sidney. She hadn't moved an inch, her arms folded over her stomach, one ankle propped on top of the other. From where I was laying, it was hard to tell if her eyes were even open. Occasionally I could hear the distant hum of a semi rolling into town. Somewhere, the rhythmic squeak of that swing chain cut through the hot air. Staring at the branches was almost hypnotic. I felt like I was just waking up. Or just falling asleep.

"Hey Sid?" I whispered again.
"Yeah?"
"I was just wondering, have you ever caught one?"
"What, an apple?" she asked softly.
"Yeah, did you or your sisters ever catch one?"
"No, not yet."

I imagined an eight-year-old Sidney in her backyard, a sister to either side, playing a game seriously the way only kids can do. I was the same way, I just played different games. When my brother and I played baseball, we weren't just playing a game in the backyard, we were the Tigers and it was Game 7 and losing was something we'd never get over, at least not until the next day when we'd play it all over again.

"How often did you and your sisters play?"
"Kaitlyn and Lindsay and I used to lay in the backyard for hours, especially when my mom first told us about it. We played just about every day that fall. Kaitlyn was only four and she would fall asleep a lot of the time, but Lindsay and I would lay for hours and sing songs, or just talk."

It was a nice memory, I didn't need to see Sidney's face to know that.

"But you've never caught one, huh?" I asked.
"No, not yet," she said again. "Actually, I've never even seen one fall."

16

"Danny, thank God you're home," Jim said, an unfamiliar panic in his voice. "Janine's in labor, how fast can you get here?"

"In labor now? It's early, isn't it?"

"Yeah, a couple weeks. Can you watch the girls?"

Less than four minutes later I turned onto the Golds' street and saw Jim pull the tailgate closed and race back toward the house. I pulled to the curb and was about to follow him inside when I noticed Janine in the passenger seat, writhing in pain. I never know what to say when something like that happens, so I continued to the porch. I don't think Janine ever saw me.

Jim was getting the girls settled on the sofa in front of the TV when I opened the door. The squeak startled him and his head spun to me, revealing a pair of moist eyes fighting to stay calm. The girls were terrified, and Jim was trying to assure them everything was fine.

"You two be good for Danny, I'll call in a little while. Everything's going to be fine."

He kissed them both quickly, then sprang toward me, continuing through the front door without pausing. I followed him off the porch and down the driveway as he barked over his shoulder.

"Can't get ahold of Mrs. T, I'll keep trying," he said. "Just need you to sit with them until she gets here. Girls ate lunch."

He pulled open the door of the Bronco, releasing the full force of Janine's cry, a piercing wail that cut across the quiet neighborhood. Jane and Lily were sitting with their noses pressed against the glass of the bay window, wide-eyed. Once inside the truck with the engine running, Jim seemed relieved. There was a calm to his hurry.

"It's gonna be OK baby, we're going," he told Janine as he shifted the truck into reverse.

"Danny," he called through the open window as he backed out of the drive. "Help yourself to anything, I'll call you in a little while. And thanks man!"

I watched Jim and Janine race off, and as the Bronco turned the corner I saw the frightened faces of Jane and Lily, still at the front window. It was a short walk up the driveway to decide what to say.

"Alright you two, this is going to be cool," is what I came up with, wearing the happiest face I could muster as I bounced into the house.

I was met by four little watery eyes staring up at me, full of questions and fear.

"Why was Mommy crying, Danny?" Jane asked, her arms wrapped tight around the chest of a stuffed animal. I led them to the couch, sat them close to one another, and knelt down in front of them.

"Everything is fine. In a little while, you two are going to have a little brother or little sister," I said, not sure where the talk was leading. "What do you think of that?"

A hint of a smile on each of their faces told me I was headed in the right direction.

"What are you hoping for, brother or sister?" I asked.

They looked at one another, as if confirming a conversation they'd already had, and then back at me.

"A brother," they said in unison.

From there, I was in the clear. We spent the evening chatting about possible names, about the girls sharing a bedroom, about how they wanted to take the baby on walks to the park. Every five minutes they whined about why it was taking so long for their Dad to call. I did my best to assure them that sometimes it takes a while, and tried distracting them with board games and snacks. Over juice boxes and an intense game of Chutes n' Ladders at the kitchen table, I learned all about Mrs. T., the older woman next door who usually steps in to watch the kids any time Jim and Janine need her. Jane and Lily were describing with no shortage of detail why Mrs. T. is so much fun. Among other things, she apparently makes the best cookies.

We were still doing battle on the game board when the phone rang a little before 9 o'clock. The three of us looked at one another for an instant, and then sprung from our chairs. The girls beat me to the phone, but waited to let me answer.

"Danny, it's Jim. Everything OK there?"

"Great, we're fine, what about there? Any news?"

The girls were clutching at my shirt, begging for info.

"It's a boy," Jim said. I could feel him gushing through the phone. "He was born about 15 minutes ago. He's great, Janine's great. Everybody's perfect."

"Excellent, congrats," I said. "Two little people here are anxious to hear. Let me hand the phone to them."

Their cheeks touching, their ears pressed against the receiver, Jane and Lily listened intently as Jim told them about their brother. Their faces lit with excitement, and shrill squeaks carried through the house. Without interrupting their celebration, I pried the phone from their hands and strolled to the porch.

"I think they approve," I told Jim. "So, give me the details, what kind of stats did the little guy put up?"

He was 7 pounds, 4 ounces, 19 inches, with a dusting of light-brown hair. Jim and Janine hadn't settled on a name, but were leaning toward Jon.

"He's perfect, man," Jim said. "Looks just like Janine. Healthy, got some meat on him. Perfect. Danny, I still haven't had any luck getting ahold of Mrs. T. You sure you're OK there? I'm not keeping you from anything?"

"Stop worrying about it, we're having a great time. Do what you need to do, stay the night at the hospital, we're fine. I already told the girls I was gonna let them cheat on their bedtime by a half-hour."

A deep chuckle was Jim's only response. The late bedtime had secured my status as one of the world's greatest babysitters, even without baking skills. And then I threw out an idea that clinched it.

"How about if I bring the girls up to meet the little guy? Just for a few minutes, then straight home to bed."

"You sure?"

"Definitely. They'll be jacked. We won't stay long, I'm sure Janine needs to rest."

"That'd be great, I'll let you tell them this time. I'll see you guys up here in a little bit then. And Danny, thanks again, for everything."

Jane and Lily were still jumping in celebration in the living room. Their high-pitched squeals reached new volume levels as they scurried around the house looking for shoes, sweatshirts, stuffed animals, blankets and who knows what else. It was really a miraculous thing to watch.

Jonathon Andrew Gold slept soundly in what looked like a large, glass casserole dish. Janine was resting comfortably in front of a small oscillating fan. Jim stared out a window overlooking the hospital parking lot, his back to the door, his arms folded over his chest.

"Anybody awake in here?" I whispered as I poked my head into the open door.

Jim turned wearing an enormous smile beneath his tired eyes.

Jane and Lily were pressing at my legs, and when I saw it was OK I let them squirt past my knees and into the hospital room.

"Hey, there are my girls!" Jim said as they exploded into his arms. He scooped up both as if he was carrying two footballs.

The girls' excitement transformed into pure wonder as Jim hoisted them high enough to see over the edge of the glass dish. Jon lay on his back, completely still except occasional quivers of his lower lip. He was wrapped tight in a light blue blanket. A powder blue hat covered his head. Jim leaned in close and their three faces splashed a genuine, pure love over Jon. From my angle, Janine was directly behind them, sound asleep with a faint smile on her face.

I pulled my camera from its case, raised it to get Jim's approval, and began taking pictures. I wanted to give Jim and Janine a framed photo as a gift. I got a picture of the girls standing on tiptoes to see their brother over the glass edge of his bed. I took one of Lily's face so close to her brother's they were practically touching. And I took countless shots of Jon, his round cheeks filling my lens.

"Daniel Evart, don't you dare aim that thing at me."

Janine's voice was a soft, crackling whisper, and hearing it sent Jane and Lily into a tear.

"Mommy!" they squealed, and leapt up on the side of her hospital bed, forming a pile as she wrapped an arm around each of them. Jim soon joined, standing bedside and leaning over the whole scene. Without Janine noticing, I managed to snap a few pictures.

As if he was being left out, Jon soon cooed, hardly enough to call a cry. His eyes were still closed tight.

Jim was immediately at his side, transferring Jon from his bed into the waiting arms of his mother and sisters. I watched briefly as the Golds took turns holding him. The expression in the eyes of Jane and Lily as they held their baby brother for the first time was like nothing I'd ever seen. It was a moment for Jim and his family, and I felt instantly out of place. Like an intruder. I motioned to Jim that I'd wait in the hallway, and slipped quietly from the room.

17

For one more day I wasn't a student and I wasn't a photographer, at least not one who worked for a newspaper. For one more day, I wasn't anything. I was just a guy with a college degree whose most pressing chore was to set a can of cat food on the porch. Mrs. T. showed up just after sunrise, and I went home to do nothing. I spent most of the afternoon sitting with Apostrophe and listening to the Tigers on the radio. By the end of the game I dialed Sidney's number for at least the 10th time, but still didn't get an answer. By early evening I was flicking whirlybirds that had begun collecting on the porch from an enormous sugar maple that stands behind the house. I'd launch them from the porch railing and watch them spin aimlessly to the gravel below.

By Monday morning I was anxious for a break from the nothing.

The *Daily Mirror* resides in an aging two-story building in the heart of downtown Wanishing, a block north of the Crow's Nest, a few blocks south of the parks and rec building. Two large windows flank the main entrance. Above the door, the newspaper's masthead is displayed in Old English-style wooden letters.

The photo department consists of three desks positioned in a U-shape, tucked into a back corner of the newsroom. A door behind them leads to the darkroom. Computers sit on two of the desks, one reserved for Peter Spellman, the *Mirror* photo editor of about two decades, and the other for whoever happens to be his only staff photographer at any given time. Spellman uses the third desk to lay out and size prints.

Before leading me back to my new work area, Corbin guided me through a personal tour of the entire building, introducing me along the way to the handful of middle-aged women who form the classified department, the pretty ex-sorority girls who comprise the ad staff, and some of the copy editors, news reporters and sports writers who happened to be in the building. After an hour-long winding tour, I found myself staring at the back of Spellman's balding head.

The old man was hard at work, sizing head shots of four Wanishing residents to be featured in "Street Beat." It's the *Mirror*'s version of a weekly feature that appears in some form in nearly every small newspaper in the world, where a reporter hits the town to ask locals a question that nobody considers important. That week's assignment sent Spellman and one of the reporters to the Shop N' Mart to flag down four people and ask them, "What's your favorite kind of pie?". One of the worst assignments you can get as a photographer is taking a picture of some lady standing there holding a bag of groceries. It's torture.

"Peter, help has arrived," Corbin announced, as if two weeks without a staff photographer had pushed Spellman to the brink of exhaustion.

The old man spun slowly in his chair, cautious not to disturb a pair of reading glasses that teetered on the tip of his nose.

"Mis-ter Ev-art," he said, the longest four syllables I've ever endured. "It's a pleasure – to have you on board."

We shook hands and I was afraid his metacarpals might crumble in my palm. Spellman walked slow, talked slower and turned what should have been a series of quick tasks into a full day's work. The funny thing is, I liked working for Spellman. My second day on the job he invited me for a beer at the Crow's Nest. Spellman enjoyed talking, and one beer lasted him nearly an hour.

Spellman moved to Wanishing from Colorado in the late '70s, a month after his wife died in a car accident. Near as I could tell, working at the *Mirror* was about all he had.

"Needed," he said, pausing to sip, "to start fresh."

He shook his head as if shaking away the memories.

"I missed the job at first, worked at a great little paper out there. But I needed a change. Friend of mine who teaches here at the college told me about an opening at the *Mirror*. Fifteen years later, here I am."

Spellman rattled off the highlights of his story the way students in a history class outline something that happened centuries ago. It bothered him inside, I could tell by how quiet he got, but he didn't well up and start crying or anything. He just changed the subject.

"So Danny, tell me what you think," he asked, "of our fine publication."

"Looks great, I love that you added more color pages," I said. "Whoever does page layout seems to like using a lot of photography, so I'm looking forward to that."

Spellman lifted his mug for another drink, and it seemed like five minutes later he put it back on the table and continued talking.

"Assignments can get stale, I'm not going to lie. Council meetings. Business development stories. Every now and then you'll get over to campus. Where we've been lacking is with features. Always keep your eyes open for features, Danny."

He stopped talking, and I sensed he was expecting me to rattle off a few ideas on the spot.

"I've got something Thursday night that might be good," I said. "A few GLU students are in a band called Bag of Hate. They're having a CD release party over at the Grapevine. Could get some great shots there."

Spellman rubbed his chin as he processed the details, then his face contorted almost painfully.

"What in the hell," he asked, "is a bag of hate?"

The two of us, separated by more than four decades, shared a hard laugh. I was laughing as much at Spellman's reaction as I was the band's name. He had a gasping, whining laugh that struggled to escape his face. Maybe he didn't do it often enough.

"Bag of hate," he repeated, shaking his head.

"So what do you think, want me to shoot it?"

Residual laughter was still leaking from Spellman's body.

"My good Lord, bag of hate," he said again. "How'd they come up with that name?"

I knew the story, the real story, but I spared Spellman the winding narrative and shrugged.

"So what do you think?" I asked again. "I'm planning on going anyway, it's no problem getting some shots."

"Why not, go ahead and shoot it. Just remember you're not on weekly deadlines any more. We need images by midnight to make Friday's paper. And I doubt we'll have a reporter there, so get what you need for a cutline."

Our conversation broke again for Spellman to have some more beer.

"So what kind of music," he continued, "does this Bag of Hate play?"

"Rock. Grunge. Pretty heavy stuff, but they're good."

Spellman chuckled again at the name, this time without repeating it.

"And how about this Franklin kid, the TV show guy. Anything we can do there?"

The *Mirror* had run "Who's Who?" updates virtually every day since breaking the news about Lydia Styles. Spellman was determined to make as much use as possible of the mountains of pictures I had from our trip to Chicago. They were probably all technically property of the *Telegram*, but I told Spellman I'd dig through what I had to see what I could come up with.

"Have you talked with him since he left?"

"A couple of times," I said. "He's having fun with it, that's for sure. He's excited."

Spellman lifted his eyebrows and whistled.

"Damn right he's excited," he said. "A quarter of million dollars. You know, I worked at the *Mirror* for more than eight years before I earned a quarter of million dollars. And he's looking at a few months? Oh, he's excited all right."

Spellman and I sat in a quiet corner at the Crow's Nest until nearly midnight, talking a little bit about work but more about life. Spellman had adopted Detroit's sports teams since moving from Colorado. He especially loved the Tigers and Red Wings. We talked about northern Michigan, which Spellman repeatedly referred to as a "hidden gem." He had never been here when he moved from out west, and he marveled at what he didn't know. And he talked endlessly about music. Spellman was a huge Elvis fan.

"Music that lasts, that's how you can tell what's good, Danny," he said. "The big-today, gone-tomorrow music, that stuff, you can keep it."

Spellman waved his thumb toward the jukebox and the Pearl Jam song that was playing.

"But, I guess you never know what will last," he said. "Forty years from now, who knows, people might be reliving the first time they heard Bag of Hate."

This set off another round of wheezing laughter. I was glad that Spellman never asked for the name of the band's new CD or titles from their track list. He might have had a heart attack right there at the Crow's Nest.

Gubble Bum is Bag of Hate's second self-recorded, self-distributed CD, and even before its official release it was being viewed as considerably more advanced than their debut album, *You and Me and Baby Makes Pee*.

According to an early review that appeared in the *Campus Telegram* the same day as our feature on Darren Morrell, "Bag of Hate's latest effort shows evidence of a band evolution in terms of song writing and musicianship." Whatever that means.

Nearly as much as the music itself, Bag of Hate continues to intrigue fans of the local music scene simply by virtue of a name that has grown mythically in three years. The stories that circulate around campus as to the origins of Bag of Hate's name are too numerous to count. Most of the rumors are clever, I'll give them that, but they're miles from accurate. I heard the real story straight from Sidney. Eb once asked the guys in the band if they minded him writing an article to tell the story. Kyle and Stelly discussed the idea briefly before requesting he didn't.

"It's kind of cool letting those urban myths grow," Stelly said.

Whether it is possible for an urban myth to exist in a city whose tallest building is three stories high, I wasn't sure, but I didn't badger him about it. Besides, I kind of agreed with Stelly. It was funny listening to people describe with certainty something that was 100 percent wrong. As good as the stories are, though, none compare to the truth.

SharLia Jackson was a highway construction worker in Detroit, tagged with one of the most anonymously visible gigs in the world. As the heavy, pavement-pounding machines operated behind her, SharLia stood in the face of rush-hour traffic holding a "slow" sign. Next to tollbooth operator, I imagine it to be one of the most miserable jobs out there. One summer day a few years ago SharLia was standing with her sign on I-75 near Tiger Stadium. The mid-morning surge of suburbanites scurrying to work had already come and gone. SharLia, according to news reports that played steadily for three days, was a 12-year road crew veteran, and a lifelong Detroiter single-handedly raising two kids on the city's east side. I had just finished my freshman year and was home for the summer. I remember watching the television anchors forcing sorrowed looks as they detailed the story.

Dale Sinclair's pickup truck was barreling up 75 toward his family's farm near Bay City. One minute he was tapping the steering wheel to the beat of a Charlie Daniels song, according to his account, and the next his face was buried in the truck's airbag. He never saw SharLia. His front bumper sent her sailing, over the median wall and into the middle of the southbound lanes. His truck, which careened off the wall before coming to rest on the side of an enormous pile of sand, was beat up pretty badly, but Sinclair, shielded by an airbag that deployed for no apparent reason, walked away with only minor scratches. SharLia died instantly.

In the aftermath, Sinclair was one of the most hotly sought-after interviews in town, and initially he was portrayed as a victim nearly as much as was SharLia. But following a formal press conference, a TV cameraman caught Sinclair on tape commenting to a friend, "at least it was only a colored girl that got kill't."

The media outcry was deafening. Dale Sinclair became the focus of countless behind-the-scenes stories. TV crews camped along the small country road that lines his family's farmhouse, eagerly waiting to get footage of the 67-year-old man doing anything worth reporting. In the end, they didn't get much, except numerous accounts that confirmed the old man was racist. By the time the story faded away, nearly anyone in the southeast corner of the state knew Dale Sinclair by face and by name. Most had forgotten all about SharLia Jackson.

That summer, Kyle, Stelly and a drummer named Griggs had been banging around on their instruments in Kyle's suburban Detroit loft. They weren't planning anything big, or even anything permanent. Their musical aspirations included little more than making a few bucks on weekends and picking up girls after the shows. For about four weeks, until a racist guy named Dale Sinclair plowed his pickup truck into SharLia Jackson, they played under the name of Pegasus.

Because I knew the real story, it was with pride that I listened as Kyle lifted the heavy swoop of hair that hangs across his face and mumbled into the microphone, "Here's a song we wrote for SharLia Jackson." Not only was the band name a tribute, they'd also written a song for SharLia. Most everybody at the Grapevine was too greased to know or care what he meant.

With that, Bag of Hate launched into "Rundown," a simple, trashy song that had become Bag's most recognizable tune around Wanishing thanks to the radio play it received on WGLU, the campus station where Griggs' roommate pretended to be a programming director. Because of the airplay, it had become the unofficial anchor of *...Baby Makes Pee.*

Kyle, a showy performer even during an average set, was in rare form at the Vine, leaping from his amplifier, climbing atop the stage-side tables and wailing wildly on his guitar. The trio stretched the typically three-minute-long "Rundown" to a 10-minute-long thrashing jubilee, confirming in the minds of the Bag faithful its anthem status. As the song wound down, concluding with all three players slamming aimlessly on their instruments, Kyle stepped to the microphone and stated somberly, "Dale Sinclair, eat my shit." It was an element lost on the studio version, but the boys had practiced it well, their instruments grinding to a halt on the word "shit." I was positioned at the edge of the foot-high stage, kneeling low and snapping pictures.

The bar exploded when the song stopped, more likely because of the fecal reference than for any political message. As the last of the guitar feedback filtered from the room, Griggs rose behind his drum kit to bask in the applause. Kyle stood tall at the lip of the tiny stage, his eyes surveying the crowd. He found Sidney sitting opposite of where I was squatting and winked.

"All right GLU!" Kyle hollered into the mic, his voice pushing the crowd quieter. "I just want to say a few words before we rip this place up right. First of all, thanks for coming to celebrate our new CD, *Gubble Bum*. Be sure to pick up a copy at the bar before you leave."

He let the crowd of 100 people chirp some more, swallowing a half bottle of beer to fuel the applause.

"But we've got more news to pass along," he continued. "What you don't know yet, because we just finalized everything ourselves earlier this week, is that this is our last show here in Wanishing for a while."

The news was greeted by a smattering of boos. I turned again to find Sidney, who was sitting at her table and clapping alongside a group of girls.

"Not only is tonight our CD release party, it's also kind of a going-away celebration," Kyle continued. "Tomorrow morning we're packing into Stelly's van and heading on a tour of bars across the Midwest."

Loud applause filled the room and Kyle swum in it.

"Don't worry, don't worry," he said. "We'll be back for winter semester, so just consider this a short break. If you graduated and are leaving town, I hope our paths cross again someday. Either way, consider this a new start for Bag of Hate. And consider tonight...ONE FOR THE FRIGGIN' RO-O-O-O-O-OAD!"

Rehearsed to precision, Griggs poured beer into his mouth with one hand, banged an increasingly faster beat with the other, and the band broke into a raucous version of "Shame On Me," another thrasher that sent the bar into an uproar. Nearly everyone packed into the Vine leaped from their seats and filled the small dance floor in front of the stage. I stayed crouched on the floor, tucked into a corner with my head pressed against an amplifier. Through the slamming bodies, flailing arms and pounding heads, my eyes found Sidney again. This time hers found mine, for only a second. I didn't need to ask and she didn't need to answer. Sidney nervously looked away, saying plenty.

Bag of Hate was going on the road, and Sidney was going with them.

18

The ringing phone pulled me from a sound sleep. I jolted upright, thinking it might be Sidney.

"D, what's happening?"

It was Eb. Darkness was just beginning to fade out my bedroom window. With the time difference, it must have been about 6 o'clock in Chicago. I moaned.

"D, you there?"

"Mm-hmm," I mumbled. "What's up Eb?"

"Doing great, but need your help. Challenge Clue."

Eb described the card, which was slipped under the door of his apartment just moments earlier. Why he was awake to receive it, I have no idea. Like the card Darren found when I was in Chicago, this one displayed the large "Who's Who?" question mark on one side. On the other was a black-and-white picture of a man's face. That was it. No fine-print line, just a picture of a guy who Eb said looked like he might be "one of those old Chicago gangster guys or something."

"You got any ideas?" he asked.

I was still brushing aside sleep, the memory of the Grapevine and a late-night trip to the *Mirror* darkroom still fresh. It felt like I'd been in bed for about 15 minutes.

"Kind of need to see it," I said. "Maybe you should try the library or something. Find out who the guy is."

Eb agreed, spent another 10 minutes trying to crack the case right there on the phone with me, then finally surrendered to the fact that I would be of no help.

"So how's Wanishing? How's the *Mirror*?"

I told him about my first week at work and about the Bag of Hate concert and how the band was leaving town for a while. He was excited at the idea of catching a show in Chicago.

"How about with you?" I asked. "How's the show going?"

The questions ignited a flurry of stories that let Eb describe filming sessions, cast member meetings, promotional responsibilities and more conversations with Stuart than he was able to count. Eb was awarded the bonus clue that Darren earned for selling the most peanuts at Wrigley, which seemed fair since Eb was actually the one who sold most of them. Even with that clue in hand, Eb said he was still no closer to finding any mystery woman.

"Between you and me, D, I think a lot of this is rigged," he said. "Feels like it, anyway. I know it's supposed to come off as this real-life, in-search-of kind of thing. But it feels like they're just waiting to decide which of us to give the info to."

I didn't say anything. My interest in the show was draining quickly. And I was so tired.

"Who the hell knows, man, maybe I'm just imagining things," he continued. "All I know is the clues I've gotten so far don't help at all."

He returned to studying the index card, I could tell because I could hear him flicking the corner of it over and over with his finger. After a few seconds, he finally broke the silence.

"Listen, I've got to run D. I've got to get down to the train station to shoot some promos. It's going to suck, they said we'll probably be there four or five hours."

"OK, call me later and we'll go over that clue some more."

We hung up and I wrestled to get back to sleep, trying hard to let a dream resume from when it was interrupted. I knew it wouldn't. Once you lose a dream like that, you can never get it back.

Scratching at the front door convinced me to give up on sleep, and I got up to find a can of food for Apostrophe. I opened the door in my underwear, holding a turkey and giblet dinner.

"Gotcha."

Sidney was wearing a baggy white sweatshirt, cutoff jeans and brown sandals. Her Apostrophe impression was impressive.

"Here you go, I hope you like it," I said, handing her the can. "It doesn't smell the greatest."

Sidney laughed, set the can under the metal bench and picked up the plastic-wrapped copy of the *Mirror* from the porch.

"I'm surprised to see you, I thought you'd be gone already."

"We're leaving in a little while," she said, closing the door behind her. "They're playing in Ann Arbor tonight."

The guys were at Stelly's figuring out ways to best fit their equipment in the back of Stelly's van. Sidney said it was going to be a tight squeeze, but they'd make it.

"I hope I didn't wake you up," she said. "Just wanted to stop by to see you before we, you know, leave."

Bag of Hate played until nearly 1:30 before the CD release party drifted over to Griggs' apartment. Sidney left at about 3 o'clock, but she said she heard there were still people awake when the sun came up.

"Where did you disappear to?" she asked.

"Had to get to the office to get the photos in for today's paper. Have you seen it yet?"

I motioned for her to open the wrapped copy. She slipped off the plastic bag and flipped the pages before stopping somewhere inside. It was a 3-column picture of Kyle, his mouth pressed against the microphone, his eyes locked tight. The extended caption gave all the details of Bag's performance at the Grapevine, including some info on the new CD and a brief mention that they were heading on a tour of bars throughout the Midwest. Sidney loved it.

"I have to get one of these before we leave. The guys are going to want to see this."

"Take that one, I can get a million at work. Really, take it."

Sidney thanked me and slid the folded up newspaper into an over-sized bag that hung over her shoulder.

During all of the time we spent sitting beneath the willow tree, all of the time we spent walking the trails around the Sands, never, not once, whether we were working on homework or talking, have I felt any awkwardness with Sidney. But that day in my apartment, the day Sidney and Bag of Hate were leaving Wanishing, something felt different. It was uncomfortable.

Sidney did her research and learned that she could return to school after Christmas and still graduate next spring, with only one class to take next summer. I showed her a picture of Jon Gold and she nearly started crying. She promised to send me postcards from the tour. I promised to look for them. We talked for a half-hour or so, but I couldn't shake the feeling that something was missing. Sadness has a way of skewing things.

"Oh, I almost forgot, I wanted to give you this," she said, digging into that enormous shoulder bag to find a folded sheet of paper. "It's the tour dates and bars for the first few weeks. I don't know if you'll need it, but you never know."

FOREVER SINCE AN APPLE

F, 8/20 & Sa, 8/21 – Sterling's, Ann Arbor
T, 8/24 – the Underground, Detroit
Th, 8/26 – Cheddar, Toledo
F, 8/27 & Sa, 8/28 – Rip Tide, Cleveland
M, 8/30 – The O Bar, Columbus
W, 9/1 & Th, 9/2 – After Hours, Dayton
F, 9/3, Sa, 9/4 & Su, 9/5 – Grooves, Indy
W, 9/8, Th, 9/9 & F, 9/10 – Sound Stage, Chicago

The dates, bar names and cities were scribbled in red pen. It wasn't Sidney's handwriting, I could tell. Probably Stelly's. Sidney promised she would keep me posted as additional tour dates were finalized.

I scanned the page as we walked onto the porch and down the steps. It was awkward figuring out where to stop. On the bottom step, I leaned against the railing and wished Sidney a good trip. She hugged me, and I hugged her back. And then I watched her leave. I sat and just watched her as she stepped across the lawn, paused to wave goodbye again and disappeared around the corner of the house. The wood of the step was warm in the morning sun. With Bag of Hate's tour calendar folded in my fingers, I leaned back and the stairs drew lines of heat across my back. I felt the warmth of the sun on my body and through my eyelids watched a yellow world wrap around me in a dizzy swirl.

When Eb left town, the apartment felt empty. He didn't take a bunch of our furniture, but the place just felt a little less lived in after he was gone. But when Sidney left, the place felt more than just empty.

When Sidney left, I felt alone.

19

A combination of no fewer than five factors led to my all-time record whirlybird launch. I struck it true, and it rose from the porch railing, lifted in a timely breeze and spun wildly as it carried over the gravel lot, over the street and over a wooden fence that lines the neighbor's yard. I watched its entire flight, and raced down the steps to follow it once it became clear that something special was happening. It finally landed in grass about six inches from a pile of dog poop. I never took an official measurement, but it had to be 35 yards.

Whirlybirds carpeted the porch by late August. That big sugar maple around back was dumping them by the handfuls. Apostrophe, if his nap stretched long enough, would wake up with little red and green paper blades stuck to his fur. The whole driveway, the whole neighborhood, was littered with them, but our second-story porch really seemed to attract them. Wind patterns, or something.

The porch railing is perfect for launching. It's built of 2x4s on their side, so I have plenty of room to make a clean strike with my fingernail, and its gray paint is glossy and smooth to allow for grab-free liftoffs.

My one-man competition began kind of by accident. On a food run for Apostrophe, I swatted a whirlybird from the railing, just because it was there. I watched it twirl and curl to the parking lot below. So I swatted another one. And I watched that one. I swatted another and another, watching each one float away, most landing somewhere in the gravel lot. Eventually I grabbed a stool from the kitchen and started gunning for distance and direction. Apostrophe might have been amused had he bothered to wake up and watch.

Sugar maple whirlybirds, although I'm pretty sure that's not their official name, are U-shaped, with a seed at the center of two paper-thin wings. I experimented with dozens of different launch techniques. Seed down. Seed up. Wings left or right. Laid flat. I flicked so many whirlybirds my finger got sore. Some, if I hit them wrong, would crumble and fall straight to the ground below the porch. Some would suffer a tear to one wing, and flutter clumsily toward the parking lot.

Every now and then I'd catch one just right. Like that record-breaker. Its seed was as heavy as an olive pit. Its thick wings were durable, probably three inches from corner to corner. It left the railing like a shot and its wings settled into a red-and-green blur, spiraling 10 feet above me before the wind grabbed ahold. It was nearly to the road and still above eye level when I knew it was worth tracking. It was airborne for what felt like five minutes, dancing above the street, fluttering. When it fell, it fell quickly but softly, just clearing the fence.

I wished Eb had been there to see it. Eb would have come up with a name for it, like "a new Whirl Record," and we would have sat on the porch for an hour laughing at other ways to describe a far-flung whirlybird. And then he would have spent the rest of the summer and fall trying to launch one further.

Wanishing is quiet during the third week of August. Summer-class students scatter to enjoy the last of summer before fall classes begin. Students who've been gone since spring don't usually come back to town until late August. The street was empty as I chased the whirlybird from my porch, and when it landed I checked to see if anybody had witnessed it. Nobody did.

20

You can only spend so much time on the porch with Apostrophe. Honestly, I don't know how Eb did it all summer. The *Mirror* office was quiet just after 6 o'clock Monday morning. Three bundles of the day's paper were stacked on the front steps. It took me five minutes to wiggle the key the right way to get the door open, and another 10 minutes to find the light switches. When I finally did, banks of aging fluorescent bulbs lit the newsroom slowly, joined by a gentle hum overhead. The smell of bleach hung in the air, residue from the weekend cleaning crew. My week was off to a glamorous start.

I went straight to Spellman's archaic assignment board, anxious to see what he had lined up for me. I was hoping to spend most of the day hunting around town for features. My name appeared next to two entries: "WMH ribbon-cutting, 1:00" and "Billboard, Old County Rd., tbd" Neither sounded too exciting, but at least they would get me out of the office. I spent the early part of the morning sizing and cropping some headshots piled in a basket on Spellman's desk, and watched the newsroom slowly come to life. By the time Spellman finally meandered in just before 9 – Spellman's arrival time was like clockwork, I learned – I had erased a stack of work that would have taken him three days to finish.

"Getting a jump on the week I see," Spellman said, a proud grin peeking behind the rim of his coffee cup.

When he finally finished taking a drink, he went into a recap of the assignment board. The 1:00 item was a simple ribbon-cutting ceremony at the newly renovated Wanishing Memorial Hospital. A grip-and-grin, Shipler would have called it.

"For the other one, you're going to have to do a little more work I'm afraid," he said. "Friend of mine owns an advertising company. He called Friday and said his crew will be putting up a billboard for that TV show. It's over on Old County Road just south of the shopping center. Supposed to go up sometime today, not sure when. You better get over there."

I must have looked confused.

"I know we're reaching, but see what you can come up with," he said. "Readers can't get enough on this TV show. Christ, I think we've used the Franklin kid's mug 10 times in the past three weeks. This billboard is going to be pretty impressive. Apparently they're using some kind of extension beams to make the sign 20 feet higher than normal."

From there, Spellman launched into the task of adding another sugar packet to his coffee. I grabbed my camera bags and started out, happy for an excuse to miss the weekly Monday morning staff meeting. Before I was out of earshot, Spellman called out.

"And Dan, the ribbon-cutting can be black-and-white, but shoot the billboard in color. It'll probably go 1-A."

The main support holding the billboard is a thick metal pole, at least a foot in diameter. A built-in ladder enclosed in metal caging climbs up the front of the pole. It's about a 20-foot climb to a platform where workers can stand to apply the signage.

Vinyl panels from the old billboard that advertised a local personal injury lawyer had already been removed when I pulled my car into a small lot not far from the base. The solid wooden facade looked strange against the cloudless blue sky. A field of tall weeds stood between me and a guy leaning on a pickup truck, apparently on break. He got back to work when he noticed me pointing my camera in his direction, and slowed again to greet me as I stepped through the weeds.

"Morning. Can I help you?" he asked.

"Hi. I'm with the *Daily Mirror*, getting some photos. When is the new sign going up?"

"The *Mirror*? Shit, I guess this is a big deal."

I don't know if he was waiting for me to confirm that, but I didn't say anything. We just stood there for a few seconds looking at each.

"Should have it up by the end of the day," he continued. "Gotta build up the frame first. My guy should be here with the cherry-picker any minute. Time we're done, you'll be able to see this from a mile away."

I nodded to show how impressed I was, and looked up at the platform and blank billboard towering above us.

"Jerry Mathews," he said, peeling off a work glove and thrusting his hand toward me. His hand, like his face, looked like tanned leather. Sprouts of graying hair shot from under his ball cap and over his ears.

"Dan Evart. Any chance I can get some shots from up there?"

"Sure, we can get you up there," he said, surveying the air around the billboard. "Like I say, we gotta hang that extension yet."

Jerry high-stepped through the weeds beneath the billboard and lit a cigarette. He was deep in thought. It was as if he suddenly was helming two projects: one to put up a new billboard sign, and a second to take pictures of the process. For two or three minutes he didn't say a word, just paced the area beneath the sign and studied the sky.

"Say, Dan, we can get you up on the platform, no problem. But we can get you a better look from up in the bucket. We can lift you way up and get you any angle you want."

With a couple of hours to kill before the ribbon-cutting, I scoured the city looking for features. A group of high school students were holding a car wash fundraiser in a grocery store parking lot. A guy was fishing in the river down at the Sands. Spellman would have been thrilled with those two shots alone. They were gravy compared to the billboard shots I was getting later in the day. I was in and out of the hospital event in 15 minutes, which gave me time to stop home and feed Apostrophe. I also wanted to check my mailbox for a postcard from Sidney. I promised her I would look for them.

The enormous white question mark stood 40 feet above the billboard platform, at least 60 feet above Old County Road. A dark-blue background contrasted with the light-blue sky. The line "Reality TV will never be the same" read below the question mark. "It all begins Tuesday, Sept. 7 at 8:00 PM" traced the bottom edge of the billboard, just above the platform where Jerry was kneeling, securing the final corner.

Jerry kept working, pretending not to notice my camera. After I snapped a few shots, he stood and swept his hands at the sign above him.

"What do you think?" he called, a bright smile covering his face. "She went up quick."

Jerry started a slow climb down the ladder, and I took a few more photos just in case. I knew I'd never use them; pictures without people are boring. Jerry's underling, a guy in his mid-20s with long, straw-colored hair covering his neck, was leaning against the cherry-picker bucket, gnawing on a bologna sandwich. He was far less impressed with the project than his boss.

"So what do you think?" Jerry repeated as he squeezed through the cage door. "Not bad, huh?"

"No, it looks great. You weren't kidding, it's huge."

Jerry laughed, a surprisingly squirrely giggle for a guy his size. In 10 years, he's probably hung and removed 40 or 50 signs from this billboard. I feel pretty safe guessing that none had him as amped up as the ad for "Who's Who?" did. Standing in knee-high grass, he lit another Pall Mall while he appraised his work overhead. There was a satisfaction in his smile, as if he'd just put the finishing touches on an historic work of art.

"What do you say, you ready to go up in the bucket?"

Jerry had done a fair amount of planning while I was gone. He motioned for the kid with the bologna sandwich to maneuver the truck to a position they had previously discussed, about 20 feet in front of the sign and another 20 feet to the side of it. The bucket sat limply over the bed.

"All the controls are at your fingertips," Jerry explained, running the finger of his glove over a panel of buttons mounted inside the bucket. "Up, down, swing left, swing right. Pretty simple stuff. Andy will be in the truck if there's a problem."

"Great, can we get you back up on the platform?" I asked, not bothering to explain my whole philosophy about pictures without people. "Just take a tool with you so it looks like you're doing installation."

Jerry leaped at the chance, and was scaling the caged ladder as I played with the controls to get a feel for them. Moving the bucket was jerkier than I'd anticipated.

"I want to start with a few from down lower," I called. "Then I'll lift it up and get some above. How high does this go?"

"It'll getcha to the top," Andy called. His sandwich was gone, and he was standing beneath the bucket with a sudden interest in the project. "Feels higher when you're up there."

I lifted myself 10 feet off the ground, nearly close enough to reach out and touch the corner of the platform. Jerry was already in character, playing the role of a guy putting up a billboard, even though he'd already finished a half-hour earlier. He swept a tool that looked like a squeegee across the vinyl surface, as if ironing it to smooth perfection. He crawled on his hands and knees as if giving a final quality inspection to the outer seams. What an actor. Jerry was loving it.

Even from my low angle I felt uneasy in the bucket. It rocked slightly every time I moved. And what had seemed like a windless morning on the ground gradually got breezier with every foot I climbed. I wasn't even halfway to the top and already I questioned whether it was worth 11 bucks an hour.

"You OK up there?" Jerry called as I glided past him on the platform.

I nodded, tightening my grip on the side of the bucket. I stopped midway up, forced myself to peek down, and spotted Andy, who was looking up from the weeds, cramming another bologna sandwich through his smile.

"Come on, take her all the way up!" he yelled in between bites.

The bucket inched higher, its arm creaking as it stretched. My eyes were locked on the top of the question mark. Anything to avoid looking down. They were nearly level with the top of the billboard when the arm reached its full extension. I inched my feet across the bucket floor hoping to find a balanced center, and the bucket rocked with every twitch. For a moment I froze, uncertain if I'd be able to lift my camera and lean over the bucket sill. I focused on the rubber-mat carpet to block out everything else.

"Everything OK up there?"

Jerry was still on the platform, anxious to continue pretending that he was doing something. I finally mustered up the strength to point my camera at the billboard and bang out a dozen shots. I slid the bucket a few feet and took another half dozen.

Confident that at least one of the shots would be good enough to dazzle Spellman, I quickly lowered myself to the truck. Andy's teeth greeted me as the bucket settled onto the bed. He could tell I wasn't too crazy about the ride.

"Higher than it looks, ain't it," he said. "I told ya."

I was thankful to be back on the ground, and anxious to drop off the color film and get back to the newsroom for some darkroom work. To gather myself, I paced through the weeds. Grasshoppers darted at my thighs. Jerry hovered above, that strange giggle raining down. After thanking him for the opportunity and promising that he could look for the pictures in the next day's *Mirror*, I started across the field toward my car. Before I got there, Jerry called out from his perch on the platform as a curl of purple cigarette smoke drifted from his hand.

"Hey Dan, don't forget," he called. "Up North Advertising!"

I guess everybody recognizes the value of good promotion.

21

Eb's phone calls were becoming more frequent, although I was rarely home to answer them. My days were filled with trips to every corner of Wanishing. It seemed every time I stopped home, my answering machine was blinking with a fresh message. Clues for the reality show were pouring in and Eb was getting increasingly excited with each one.

"D, I think I'm onto something. Call me," he chirped on one message.

As GLU students gradually returned to Wanishing, "Who's Who?" became the focus of conversation, spurred by the fact that a skyscraping billboard greeted most of them as they arrived back to campus. Radio and TV stations in the area talked about it constantly. And the *Mirror* did its part. Corbin made a point to get a reality TV-related story on the front page nearly every day. Spellman and I were running low on photo ideas. Soon, the *Campus Telegram* would add a fresh voice to the conversation.

Contact with Eb gave me an insider's view that was both compelling and annoying. It was impossible to not get swept up in Eb's excitement, particularly when we actually talked. And in a way, even listening to his messages confirmed my spot in a somewhat exclusive club. But at the same time, it was excruciating standing in line at a grocery store, or over-hearing women in the *Mirror* break room, yammer on despite knowing so little about it. And there I was contributing to the constant hum by feeding Corbin and Spellman a steady flow of images.

"Danny, what did you do, sleep here last night?" Spellman was still acclimating to my long work days. "Better be careful kid, don't burn out."

All the same, he seemed genuinely pleased to have the bulk of his day sorted out for him before he even parked his car in the lot. It left him time to give full attention to tasks like adding the perfect blend of cream and sugar to his endless supply of coffee.

"You get that note I left you?" he asked.

Matt Lawson is a reporter for the *Campus Telegram*, one of the small group of go-getters who returned to campus early to prepare for the school year's debut edition. He had left a message on my answering machine at home, and another at the newsroom. I assumed he wanted me to put him in contact with Eb. Asking for my help seemed a somewhat odd request, given the friendly rivalry that exists between the *Telegram* and the *Mirror*. Actually the rivalry only exists in the minds of the *Telegram* staff. From what I can tell, Corbin, Spellman and everybody else at the *Mirror* never give the *Telegram* a second thought.

"The message is already in the garbage," I said.

Spellman just chuckled and shook his head.

"So what do you have lined up today?" he asked. "Assignment board is pretty thin, got anything in mind?"

"Students are starting to trickle in, that's a possibility," I said. "A couple other things I shot yesterday, I'll get you some prints. Other than that, I'll get out and see what I find; thought maybe I'd take care of 'Street Beat' this week."

Spellman's salute and tongue-click was as official as his approvals ever got.

Apostrophe was swatting futilely at a butterfly in the yard when I rolled into the lot. A car across the street with the hatch open told me a new neighbor had arrived, but otherwise the street was as quiet as it had been all summer.

A red "2" blinked on the answering machine. The first message was from Lawson, who again didn't bother to specify why he was calling. I deleted it. The second was from Eb, whose comment was as brief as always.

"D. It's getting intense. Call me."

I did, but he didn't answer.

Back outside, Apostrophe had given up on the butterfly. The mailbox was empty.

Spellman is the type of guy who brainstorms for feature ideas by sitting as his desk with a pencil and paper. There are a lot of people in journalism like Spellman. I've never understood it. Usually they wind up with a predictable list of boring assignments. I've always found you just need to get out and look around.

I had a couple of hours to kill before meeting a reporter on campus to shoot 'Street Beat', and I decided to search on foot. Sometimes when you're driving you miss too much. I wound up a few blocks from my apartment at a small park, where two old guys were sitting at a picnic table playing chess. They each wore a wide-brimmed hat to shield the sun, and a short-sleeved button-up shirt that exposed tan, wrinkled forearms. Each had a golf ball-sized wad of chewing tobacco tucked behind his lower lip, and insisted on spitting it out before I took any pictures. Turned out they're brothers. They're 80-something Wanishing natives, and they spend every Wednesday during the summer playing chess at the park. Been doing it for 20 years. Shooting over the shoulder of one of them, I captured the other one as he moved a rook. Simple stuff, but I'll be honest, it was a great picture. I sat there and watched those two guys play chess for more than an hour. They didn't seem to mind having a spectator, even after I put my camera back in its case. I think they were happy they could chew more tobacco.

The walk the rest of the way to campus was a comfortable one, nothing like the heat romp that Eb and I had endured a few weeks earlier. It was reassuring to know that summer was into its slow fade. Outside of the Snack Shack I met Sarah Jacoby, the reporter who was handling 'Street Beat.' She was pretty fired up about the assignment.

"So what's the big question this week?" I asked, glancing around for students but finding little evidence of life.

"We're going with, 'Why are you excited about watching 'Who's Who?'," she said. "I know it presumes that people will watch the show at all, but I don't want to ask a 'Yes, No' question."

Sarah seemed genuinely proud of her clever way around the dilemma. We strolled across campus and finally found a few pockets of people. After the first guy, whose answer was a simple, "I'm not," it didn't take long to find four people who were genuinely geared up for the show. Two claimed it was going to be exciting watching someone from Wanishing on TV, even though they didn't know Eb. Another gushed that it looked like the best concept ever for a TV show. The last said she had a class with Eb and was rooting for him. All four were giddy with excitement, partly because of the TV show, partly because their picture was going to be in the paper.

It was the first time I'd walked across campus since that final poetry class. After the 'Street Beat' assignment was done, I walked south, not really looking for anything. I was just walking. I could see the willow tree from 50 yards away, and suddenly I was anxious to peek under it again. I'm not sure what I expected to find. I just wanted to see it again. I was nearly out of breath when I swept the branches aside and stuck my head inside. It felt like I hadn't been there in months. It was quiet under there, and the grass where Sidney and I used to sit was still matted. I wondered if other people had discovered it and used it as their own escape, but I dismissed that idea. I like thinking that nobody else even knows about the clearing under the willow tree, that somehow, even just a few feet from one of the busiest walkways on campus, it's a place that nobody else has discovered. Somehow it feels better that way.

I didn't stay long, knowing I had to walk back to my apartment to get my car. The walk wouldn't have taken too long had I not been stopped.

"Mr. Evart, what an unexpected pleasure?"

It was Shipler. I couldn't believe it at first. I kind of assumed he would be busy accepting a Pulitzer by then.

"Hi Aaron," I said. I hate running into people and not knowing what to say.

"How nice to see you," he said. "I trust life at the *Mirror* is treating you well?"

"Not bad, keeping busy," I said. "How about you, what are your plans?"

"I leave tomorrow, starting in a couple of weeks down at the *Free Press*. The big time."

We stood there for 10 minutes while Shipler provided me with a thorough update on where some of the other *Telegram* staffers were working. Some had scattered to newspapers across the state. Some were still looking. Schwartz took a job in Detroit at *The News*. Shipler had the entire roll call put to memory, and made a point to mention that he provided references for a handful of them. Anything to feel important. By the time he was done charting the career paths of our former colleagues, I was reprimanding myself for taking that walk across campus.

"Hey, pretty exciting about Ebner, huh?" Shipler said, his *Telegram* recap complete. "Remarkable the way that unfolded, wasn't it?"

I agreed.

"It's interesting how a chain of events can be so unpredictable."

He paused to bask in the high philosophy of his comment.

"And just think, if I had given that assignment to someone else, this whole thing wouldn't have happened."

It was right about then that I told Shipler I had to get back to work. Some people are impossible.

22

The phone was ringing when I walked through the door at 11 o'clock after a few late beers with Spellman at the Crow's Nest. I assumed it was Eb. I feared it was Lawson. I hoped it was Sidney.

"Danny, how's it doing?"

It was Jim.

"Hey, how's it going? What, is Janine having another baby already?"

Jim choked out a laugh but was clearly charged up about something else.

"Listen, I've got something for you," he said, his voice bubbling. "You free in the morning?"

I was.

"Can you meet me down at the Sands? Say around 7 o'clock?"

"Sure, what's up?"

"I'm gonna save that for the morning. Just meet me down there, this is pretty cool."

We didn't talk long, because I knew what Jim's schedule was like since Jon was born. Immediately I was anxious for morning. Just as I hung up the phone it rang again. Immediately I could hear at least a six pack in Eb's voice.

"D, holy shit, you answered. Where you been?"

"Hey Eb. Working a lot. How's it going down there? Sounds like you found something."

"Oh yeah, I'm on to something," he said. "Write this down. 'CWT806'."

I did. I had no idea why, but Eb was bursting to explain.

"They give us these pictures, one at a time, different places around the city," he said. "The first one was of the Sears Tower. So everybody leaves the theater and races over to the Sears Tower. And then we get there and we're all standing around, looking around the lobby, riding up to the observation deck. Nobody is sure what to do. We're just scurrying around the building like idiots. I'm sure there were a dozen cameras following us."

I could tell Eb was pacing around his apartment while he talked. He was pretty dialed up.

"A few days later they give us a picture of the Hancock Tower. Same deal, everybody rushes over there and then stands around not sure what to do"

"Maybe they're just trying to get you guys out in public," I said. "So they can plant cameras and get video."

"No, just wait. I figured it out. The next picture comes and it's of this old house, looks like an ancient castle.

None of us knew what the hell it was. So I run outside and start asking people on the street. I finally talk to this old guy who says it looks like the Elam House. Used to be an old boarding house for black women, like 70 or 80 years ago. I finally find out where the place is, but when I get there, there's nothing. Nobody's around."

Eb was rolling.

"I've got all this stuff tacked up on one wall in my apartment. Pictures, index cards, notes, I even went out and bought a huge map of the city. I've got all kinds of stuff up there, it looks like I'm doing some kind of criminal investigation. A few nights ago it hits me. Maybe these places don't mean shit. Maybe it's their names that are important. I noticed that the first letters of each place spelled 'S-H-E.' I figured I might be on to something. The next picture comes and it's the Delaware Building, this old building downtown. Took me awhile to figure out that one too. Last night we got another one and guess what it is. It's a headshot of Ditka."

Eb paused, waiting to see if I could catch up to him on my own. I couldn't.

"You don't see it? 'S-H-E-D-D'. The Shedd Aquarium. So this morning I fly over there. It didn't even occur to me that I didn't know what I was looking for, I just wanted to get there. When I did, it was the same thing. People everywhere, women everywhere, but none of the other guys from the show. The place is huge, and I'm standing there looking around like a moron. I have no idea what to do. So I'm outside having a smoke next to this big concrete landscape box full of flowers. I'm serious, if I hadn't stopped for a smoke there's no way I would have seen it. In with the flowers I see this little white card on a plastic stick stuck in the dirt. There's a blue question mark on the card. I couldn't believe it at first. Honestly, the first thing I did was look around for cameras. I'm sure they were there. So I grab the card and on the other side it says 'CWT806'."

Eb fell silent as he drained his beer.

"So what do you think, any ideas?" he asked after a deep swallow.

"I don't know, maybe a license plate?"

Eb considered that thought in silence.

"Possible. It made me think of something you'd see at the airport. A flight number or something."

The gears in Eb's head were really cranking. He kept whispering 'CWT806' to himself. I could hear bottles clinking in the background.

"I don't know, man, but I'm figuring this out tonight," he said. "The way I see it, I've got the lead. And I plan on keeping it."

Eb and I talked for another half-hour. He asked about Wanishing and the *Mirror*, but the conversation got jerked back to "Who's Who?" anytime something popped into Eb's mind. It was hard to blame him.

"You know, I figure they have to replace that card I took, to make sure one is there for the next guy. I'm gonna go back over there tomorrow and see. If there's one there, I'll take it. Might as well screw with 'em."

Since that moment, I've had little doubt that Eb will win "Who's Who?". He's a pretty competitive guy, and he has the personality of someone you would expect to do something like win a reality TV show.

It was after midnight when I finally remembered to check the mailbox. In a matter of seconds, I forgot all about CWT806.

Hi Dan,
Hope everything is good in Wanishing. The show in Detroit last night was great. Big crowd, and the band sounded excellent. Nice picture in the newspaper this morning, I'll save a copy for you. (Your picture is better.) How is the Mirror? I couldn't believe it, I saw you and Ebner on a TV commercial last night. You're a star! Gotta run, we're leaving for Ohio in a little while, plus I'm running out of room on this postcard.
Miss you,
Sidney
P.S. - Say hi to Apostrophe

23

The tips of Jim's boots were at the edge of the water. His hands were tucked deep in the pockets of his tan jeans. His eyes were fixed on the bend in the river when I walked up the path behind him.

"Morning stranger." My voice carried across the quiet water and bounced among the trees on the other side.

"Danny, how's it doing?" Whatever thoughts had filled his head disappeared, and his face came to life. "Thanks for meeting so early. Wait until you see this."

Jim began a brisk walk along the river's edge, following it across the beach and into the brush that fades gradually to dense woods. We tight-roped our way about 50 yards downstream, balancing on a thin plank of sand that runs between ankle-deep water on one side and elevated ground and trees on the other. As I followed Jim's steps, I watched tadpoles scurry just below the river's surface.

"Fisherman called this in yesterday," Jim explained. "Just about the time I was leaving the office, he calls and says, 'You have to come down and see this.' He was pretty bent up about it."

"What is it?"

"It's right up here. You aren't gonna believe it."

Another 10 yards up I spotted an orange five-gallon bucket sitting upside-down. "WP&R" was stamped on the side in black lettering. A couple of feet upstream, a small piece of plywood standing on end jutted from the river to divert water.

"Take a look," Jim said, bending down to lift the bucket. "Tell me what you think made this."

Jim tossed the bucket into the trees, revealing a paw print in the sand. It was clearly from the paw of a cat. A big cat. The sand was only slightly moist and had started to harden into a perfect cast. I studied it closely as I fumbled with the latch on my camera case.

"What the hell is it from?" I asked.

"Not sure, maybe a cougar. DNR will be here in a bit to check it out, but that's my best guess."

"A cougar? In Wanishing?"

"You never know, we hear about sightings," Jim said. "I've never seen one myself, but look at that thing. If not a cougar, what, a panther maybe? It's no housecat, I know that much. Obviously not a deer or a fox. I don't know what else it could be."

I inspected the print through the lens of my camera, bending low to give perspective to its size. With the camera practically sitting on the ground and my knees sinking into the damp where sand meets water, I snapped off a few shots. Morning sunlight bounced off the gently flowing river in the background. Already, I could hear Spellman gushing.

"Hey Jim, do you have a pencil or a coin or something that I can set next to it?" Jim was hovering over my shoulder trying to stay close without bothering the shot. "Something that helps show how big it is?"

"I'll do you one better," he said, digging into his vest pocket. "How will this work?"

I dropped back to my spot on the ground and banged out a few more shots while Jim leaned his arm into the picture holding a tape measure. Maybe for a day the front page of the *Mirror* would forget about reality television.

"When is the DNR coming?" I asked.

"Should be here within an hour. You need to talk to them?"

"Not so much me, but Corbin will want to get a reporter down here. I'll run to the office now to see who's around, tell them what's going on. They'll probably want to talk to you and the fisherman too."

Morning continued its slow crawl over the Sands. Shards of sunlight found their way through the trees and cast streaks of light across the river. Jim returned the bucket to its place over the paw print and we began tracing our steps up the edge of the river. During the short walk we forgot about cougars and paw prints, and fell into more familiar conversation. The kids keep

Janine and him busy. Jon gets everybody's full attention, especially the girls. Whenever Jon naps, Jane and Lily pester to wake him up, mostly because they enjoy the challenge of getting him to sleep.

"It's a funny cycle," Jim chuckled.

Once back to the Sands, I didn't stop to chat for too long. Jim said he'd keep an eye out for a reporter. We promised another bonfire before we lost summer for good. When I left him, he had returned to his spot at the river's edge, his hands pressed deep into his pockets. The river came softly around the bend, hardly moving at all.

⁂

Wanishing felt small that day. Smaller than usual. I raced from one end of the city to the other, stopping at the office to talk to Spellman, home to check the mail, back to the Sands for a few more shots with the DNR, over to campus for a shoot, back downtown for a few headshots. It had only been a week, but I'd gotten used to jamming my days with as many assignments as possible. Everywhere I went felt close.

Maybe it's because, lately, everywhere I go people are talking about "Who's Who?". Sometimes I just overhear a conversation, especially near campus. The rush of students getting back to town is in full force, and it seems every one of them stakes some kind of claim to having a relationship with Eb.

"He was in my bio class."
"We used to hang out at the bar."
"He dated my roommate two years ago."

Everybody has a story to tell, a connection to brag about. Other times people who know I'm friends with Eb come right out and ask me about the show. Usually they want to know if I think Eb will win.

After 12 hours of darting around Wanishing, ripping through rolls and rolls of film in the darkroom, writing cutlines and keeping Spellman up to speed on everything that was happening, I was looking forward to getting home, checking my messages from Eb and fading to sleep to a Tigers game. The premiere of "Who's Who?" was less than a week away, and Eb was calling on the hour, it seemed, with updates. I was almost never home to answer. By the end of the day, I might have a dozen messages waiting for me. The sun was fading when I pulled into the lot behind the apartment.

"Are you Daniel?"

The kid was sitting on the bottom step outside my apartment. His white golf shirt accentuated dark brown freckles that littered his skinny forearms. A shock of orange hair spilled off his head and draped the sides of his face. A reporter's notebook sat next to him on the step.

"Daniel, my name is Matt Lawson, I'm a reporter for the *Campus Telegram*," he began, standing to greet me with a handshake. "I'm working on a story on 'Who's

Who?' and was hoping you had a few minutes. I've left you a few messages."

"Yeah, sorry about that. I've been pretty busy."

Lawson shook his head as if to dismiss any need for an apology.

"So, I'm guessing you want me to, what, help put you in touch with Ebner?"

"Well, if you could, yes, that would be great," he said. "But somebody else is working on that story. If you have his phone number, I'll pass it along. I was actually hoping to write a story on you. You know, since you were there and all. I've seen the commercial that you're in."

The request caught me off guard. Lawson stood there fidgeting with his pen, wearing an uncomfortable grin. I was so hungry.

"Me?" I asked. "There's not much of a story really. I was only down there for a couple of days. Just working."

Lawson looked instantly dejected. I felt bad for him.

"OK, well, do you mind if I just ask you a few questions? Find out about your trip?"

I really didn't feel like arguing with him. Plus, you should have seen how pitiful he looked. For a minute, I thought he was going to start crying. Without promising a full interview, I invited him inside, emphasizing that I only had a few minutes. He didn't waste any time settling onto the couch, immediately flipped open his notebook and got in position to scribble. Then he sat there and looked at me for 30 seconds, apparently waiting for me to launch into a narrative.

"So what do you want to ask me?" I asked, interrupting a dreadful silence.

"Well, can you tell me anything about the show? You know, any behind-the-scenes stuff?"

What an interviewer. Lawson was so nervous he could hardly string together coherent sentences. Purposely avoiding any details that would be particularly interesting, I gave Lawson a five-minute recap of our trip to Chicago. I didn't mention Wrigley Field or Thad McCormick or Stuart. I especially didn't mention the dozens of messages I'd gotten from Eb, or the clues he was gathering.

"Have you talked to Ebner much since he left?" Lawson asked, flipping to a fresh page in his notebook. I have no idea what he was writing. I hadn't said one interesting thing.

"He calls once in a while," I lied as the answering machine blinked '14' on the counter. "Seems to be enjoying it."

"How about Darren Morrell? How's he doing?"

"Recovering, from what I hear. I haven't talked with him, but I heard the surgery went well."

"When you guys were down there, did anything happen with Ebner? I mean, do you know why they picked him to replace Darren?"

"Did anything happen? No, we were just working. As far as why they picked Eb, I don't know. They needed a replacement."

Lawson nodded, as if finally getting to the bottom of a daunting mystery.

"Man, he had to be surprised when they called him. How did that happen? Did they just call him out of the blue one day?"

I nodded.

"Were you with him when he got the call?"

I nodded again.

"Did you guys expect anything like that to happen?"

"Did I expect Darren's sister to go into kidney failure?" I said. "No."

"No, I mean, after you guys went down there, did you talk at all about how cool it would be to be on a show like that?"

"Nope. Like I said, we were just working, covering it. I never once thought about being a cast member."

Lawson was writing furiously.

"How about now? Now that Ebner is on the show, do you kind of wish they had called and asked you to replace Darren instead of him? I mean, that's a lot of money."

The answering machine kept blinking at me. The Tigers were already in the seventh inning. And like I said, I was starving. I shook my head and explained to Lawson that I didn't think a story on me would be a good idea. He sulked a little as I walked him to the door, but I didn't budge. Listening to people talk about "Who's Who?" was already taking up enough of my time. Appearing next to Eb in one of the TV promos didn't help. All I needed was a newspaper story that invited more questions. As

Lawson walked down the steps and disappeared around the corner of the house, I kind of felt bad for him.

I went back in the apartment and pressed the play button on my answering machine. All 14 messages were from Eb. Most were the typical variety, just messages to call him back. In one, Eb explained that CWT806 sent him to the water tower on Michigan Avenue. In others, he talked about developments with the show. Each message stretched longer than the previous, and Eb talked faster as they went. He was getting pretty jacked, it was obvious. By the 14th message, it sounded like he might climb through the phone.

"D, you aren't gonna believe it. I found her. You gotta call me. I was right, man, it's rigged. But I found her. I'm not sure what the hell's going on, but I think I might win this thing."

I turned on the Tigers game to catch the last few innings and didn't watch one pitch. All I could think about was "Who's Who?" and Eb winning. The show hadn't started airing yet, but in my mind it was over. Eb didn't answer when I returned his calls. I fell asleep on the couch imagining what would have happened if I had played those messages when Lawson was there. The kid would have had the story of a lifetime.

24

Freedom Park awoke early as Wanishing prepared for its annual Labor Day weekend festival. Tables wrapped around the outer edges of the main pavilion that hosted the headline activities. A second, smaller pavilion to the side housed a bank of kegs and wine bottles. A wooden gazebo 30 yards away was outfitted with amplifiers, drums and guitars.

For more than four decades, Wanishing has celebrated the close of one season and the arrival of a new one with Cider-Fest. GLU students are back to town in full numbers, more than doubling the city's population. Crisp autumn air completes its takeover of August's heat. Overnight, the change is unmistakable. The three-day gathering includes games for kids, beer and wine for adults and bad live music for anybody who cares to listen. I covered Cider-Fest last year for the *Campus Telegram*, and even though the festival is geared more for Wanishing locals than for college students, it's pretty good fun.

Even after my second straight week of 14-hour days, I convinced Spellman that I could spend the better part of the weekend at the park. I showed up Saturday morning tired from a week of long hours at work and late nights on the phone with Eb. The season premiere was only three days away and he was feeling pressure. Pressure from what, I was never clear.

Festival organizers were still setting up when I arrived at the park a little after 7 o'clock. A train of people were hard at work moving bushel baskets full of apples from a trailer to the main pavilion. There were thousands of apples. Some would be harpooned with wooden sticks and dunked in caramel. Some would be squeezed for every drop of juice and sold in gallon jugs. Some would be cored and sliced and sprinkled with cinnamon. Some would simply be eaten. The largest ones, though, were placed in a bin and saved for the annual apple-carving contest. In Wanishing, the apple-carving contest carries with it enormous importance. You wouldn't believe the amount of time some people put into carving an apple. Especially kids. I've heard stories of kids spending three or four hours on their project before submitting it to the contest overseer, an aging woman who sprays each entry with a solution of water and lemon juice. Apparently it keeps the apples from turning brown.

"Danny!"

Lily spotted me from 50 yards away. She and Jane broke into a sprint, leaving Jim, Janine and Jon in their wake as they rushed toward me. I managed to swing my camera bag to avoid the crushing blow of the girls leaping up and wrapping around my neck and shoulders. Their momentum pushed me back and the three of us tumbled into the grass.

"Danny, Jon's here! Jon's here!" Lily squeaked. "It's his first Cider-Fest!"

"Can you get his picture Danny? Can you get one of all three of us?"

The girls were in festival high-gear early. I imagined a non-stop day for Jim and Janine, followed by a quiet, nap-filled evening.

"Easy girls, don't hurt him," Jim said, one hand holding Janine and the other carrying Jon in a car seat. "He's getting old."

The girls climbed off me and darted immediately under the pavilion to inspect the work. They seemed to approve.

"The bosses are here early," I said, brushing leaves from my jacket. "They'll whip this thing into shape."

"Oh yeah, they know the drill," Jim said.

"Danny, I loved your picture of the paw print the other day," Janine said. "The girls cut it out and hung it on the fridge, right along with about a dozen of your other pictures."

I liked the image of the girls clipping my photos from the paper.

"You're here early too," Jim said. "Never a dull moment, huh?"

"Yeah, I'll be here most of the day. I'll keep a watch for the girls, get some pictures. And how about this guy, is he ready to carve yet?"

Jon was asleep in his car seat, hidden beneath about five pounds of fabric. Jim lifted the corner of a blue fleece blanket to reveal a pile of cheeks. Janine smiled.

"I don't think he's ready for a knife just yet," she said, relieving Jim of the car seat. "I'll catch up to the girls. Give you two a minute to plan your next bonfire."

Jim and I watched her stop every five or six feet to let women peek under the blanket.

"They're keeping you busy, huh?" Jim asked.

"I was about to say the same thing," I said. "But yeah, been putting in a lot of hours. Fine with me, not much else to do anyway."

Jane and Lily were busy under the pavilion helping sift through the bushel baskets. Janine was letting women slobber all over Jon. Jim took the opportunity to tuck a pinch of chewing tobacco in his lower lip.

"I don't know about you, but a bonfire doesn't sound bad," he said. "What do you say, next Friday night? One more before we run out of warm nights."

That quickly, the plan was cemented, and Jim and I were soon pulled into duty in different directions. Jim was called to settle a debate as to where a cotton candy machine should go. I got to work shooting pictures of two women who were setting up a huge cauldron of caramel.

I ripped off a few shots with my camera practically dipped in a big vat of brown sugar while I listened to the women chirp about the GLU student who was going to be on a reality TV show. They couldn't wait to watch.

By 10 o'clock, the festival was in full swing. Kids swarmed the pavilion anxious to snag a choice apple. It was serious business. Jane and Lily identified two supple selections and stashed them behind the gazebo. They were saving their carving for later in the day. By mid-afternoon, a bank of hay bales in the center of the pavilion would serve as a shelf to showcase everybody's work. People could wander through the rest of the evening and cast a vote for any number of category winners.

Tyler Brennan, an eight-year-old kid with a mop of blonde hair that hangs like a curtain over his forehead and ears, handled his knife like a skilled craftsman. I could tell the minute I saw his face, Tyler was intent on winning, and he began work on his apple with surgical precision. He was deliberate with every cut, working from a blueprint that hung somewhere in his mind.

I positioned myself at a table across the pavilion. I didn't want him knowing I was shooting. Whenever someone knows a camera is on them, everything changes. A group of teenagers nearby were raving about "Who's Who?". One of them was bragging that his older sister's friend knows Eb. It was getting hard to ignore. I zoomed in and got close to Tyler's face. His eyes were locked on his fruit with intensity. His tongue poked from his lips as he worked. Seeing it knocked me backwards.

The image shot through my camera lens and slammed me in the face. I had seen the picture before. I don't just mean a picture that reminded me of it, or a picture of a kid who looked like Tyler. I had seen the exact image before. The kid. The apple. The knife. The tongue. It was identical. If I didn't know better, I'd say it was a picture I took a year earlier for the *Telegram*. The familiarity left me dizzy and disoriented, and I grabbed the edge of a picnic table to keep from falling.

I wanted away from Freedom Park, away from Cider-Fest, away from little kids with knives, away from people tingling at the thought of seeing somebody they don't even know star on a reality TV show that hadn't even aired yet. That's when I realized it. I was a rounder. That's what Eb used to call it. Eb vowed that he would never land at a smalltown newspaper covering the same events year after year. The same parades. The same festivals. The same stories about kids surviving a hot summer by splashing in a water fountain, or greeting a season's first snowfall by frolicking in banks of snow.

"It's the same damn thing over and over," Eb once said. "No way am I gonna be a rounder."

And there I was. After only two weeks at the *Daily Mirror*, I was a rounder. I slung my camera case over my shoulder and hurried across Freedom Park toward the parking lot. I didn't look back to say goodbye to Jim. I didn't stop to get any final shots for Spellman. I didn't look back for anything. I just left.

25

Spellman said it was burnout, but I knew better. There was no point in arguing with him about it. When I called him Saturday evening, he insisted I take the rest of the weekend off, plus a couple of days after Labor Day. He said I had earned it. I've never spent so much time doing nothing. At least not by myself.

Apostrophe came and went, apparently sharing my inability to fill his time productively. And because of the holiday I had to endure two straight days with no mail.

I finally connected with Eb, who was as confused as he was ecstatic. He said after their weekly cast member meeting, Stuart pulled him aside and led him on a walk across town. Twenty minutes later they wandered into an Italian restaurant just off Michigan Avenue.

"He was acting weird the whole time," Eb said. "He was talking, but it was like he was just killing time."

Stuart and Eb walked straight to a table reserved in the back of the restaurant. Drinks arrived without Stuart ever ordering, and food followed.

"The whole time, he's looking around the restaurant like he's expecting something to happen," Eb said. "The minute the waitress brings our food, he changes."

Eb was pacing around his apartment as he recounted the story, I could tell.

"He whispers, 'Ebner, you do know that you're miles ahead of everybody else. Nobody's even close,' so I say, 'That's cool, but I still have no idea who this woman is,' and he says, 'The thing about this show is, you never know who might introduce you to her.'

"He says that and he stuffs a piece of garlic bread in his mouth and he stares at me, which is weird by itself. You remember his glasses? Anyway, the waitress – who's smokin' hot, by the way – she brings over more drinks and he rolls his eyes toward her and stares at me again."

"So Stuart just told you who she is?" I asked.

"He didn't tell me that he was telling me," Eb said, "but he was telling me. While we sat there eating, he kept dropping in lines like, 'She could work anywhere, at a bank or department store or museum. Or a restaurant.'

"Finally I came right out and asked him, 'Are you saying that that's her?' He just stared at me for a few more seconds and then got up to use the bathroom."

Eb's voice sounded almost scared.

"And here's the really strange part. He never came back. A waiter finally came over, asked if I needed anything else, and told me the meal was taken care of. Stuart left. And so did that waitress."

Eb and I sat silent for a minute, absorbing the details of his story. I was trying to make sense of why Stuart would just trash the whole premise of the show.

"So what are you gonna do?" I asked.

"I don't know. I went back over there this morning but the restaurant wasn't open yet. I'm going back in a little while. I'm not sure what I'll say if she's there."

I split my time the rest of the weekend between imagining what Eb was doing at the restaurant and getting the real story from him on the phone. We were on the phone last night talking about it. Eb's getting pretty jacked about the premiere. The cast is gathering tonight to watch a private screening, followed by a closed cast-member party at a bar downtown. Eb invited me to the after-party. I told him I'd try to make it.

⁂

When Spellman didn't show up for work by 9 o'clock this morning, Corbin thought it was odd. When Spellman still wasn't there by 9:30, Corbin was concerned. By 10 o'clock he was in an absolute panic and drove to Spellman's house to check on him.

Spellman passed away in his sleep last night. Corbin found him lying in bed, his TV still tuned to the channel that showed the Tigers game last night. The early word was an apparent heart attack.

I was sitting on the porch with Apostrophe waiting for the mail when Corbin called.

"Daniel, it's Larry," he said. "I know you're out of the office for a couple of days, but I'm afraid I have some bad news."

The world around the porch spun as I listened to the words. The light-blue sky, the green of a nearby maple tree, the gray stones of the parking lot swirled around me in a dizzying portrait. Spellman couldn't be dead.

"Daniel, are you still there? Daniel?"

I jerked when I returned to Corbin's voice, and Apostrophe rolled, stretched and resettled at my side.

"Yeah, sorry," I said. "I'm here."

"Daniel, I know you and Peter have become close in a fairly short time. He was a dear friend to us all. Are you OK?"

A whirlybird spun from the sky gently and landed on my foot.

"Yeah, it just doesn't seem..."

"I know," Corbin said, "it doesn't seem possible."

Corbin went on to describe how the *Mirror* staff was in a state of shock, the entire operation paralyzed. But he also emphasized that Spellman would never want to disrupt the production of the newspaper. That's just the kind of newsman Spellman was.

"Larry, is there anything I can do?" I asked. "Do you need me in there?"

I could hear Corbin rubbing his temples through the phone.

"Don't worry about it, we've got art to get us through the next couple of issues. But Daniel, and I don't want to sound insensitive here, we'll need to replace him, is the photo editor position something you're interested in? Think about it and we'll talk Thursday morning."

I hung up the phone, stood and circled aimlessly on the porch, unsure what to do or where to go. So I did nothing and went nowhere. Instead I just sat again next to Apostrophe and thought of Spellman. I laughed quietly to myself when I remembered his reaction to first hearing about Bag of Hate. I imagined the number of photos he published over a career that spanned decades, and wondered if there are still people in Colorado who remember him.

And then I cried.

I cried because Spellman was a generous man and a good boss, in some ways my mentor and in other ways my student. I think he would agree that. I cried because Spellman seemed alone, the life he really wanted long ago taken from him. As I cried I realized that, in just two weeks Spellman had become my friend.

I was still on the porch when the paper boy hurried past and fired a rolled up copy of the *Mirror* up the steps. It landed two steps below me.

I knew that Corbin had prepared a special front-page feature to preview the "Who's Who?" premiere, but I opened the paper anyway. The front page is a poster of

Eb, a blown-up reprint of a picture I took when we were in Chicago. The headline reads *"SHOW TIME!"* in letters so big I could have read it from across the street. The story talks all about how Eb managed to drift from a city in eastern Pennsylvania to a small town in northern Michigan to a starring role on a reality television show. The article is well written, but it was hard for me to get through since I knew so much more of the story.

I was looking at the *Mirror* but thinking about Spellman when the mailman bounded up the steps. Dark sunglasses covered the top half of his face, and a scraggly goatee the bottom. Every inch of his forearms was covered by tattoos. Headphones from his Walkman covered his ears.

"How's it going, man," he said, almost yelling. "Hey, cool looking cat."

I almost said "thank you" before realizing he wouldn't hear me. Besides, there wasn't any reason for me to take credit for Apostrophe.

He rifled through his bag for our mail and emerged with a handful of envelopes and cards. As he stretched from his spot on the steps halfway up, he noticed the name on one of the envelopes.

"Hey, is this the dude who's going to be on that reality show?" He was still hollering.

When he couldn't hear my answer, he pulled the headphones down around his neck.

"Yeah, that's him," I repeated.

"I read about him. Man, is that dude lucky or what?"

I didn't disagree.

"Dude can just chill in Chicago for a while and bask in the royal treatment, you know what I'm saying?" he said. "It beats hauling this bag around all day. People keep saying, 'If he wins, if he wins.' Shit, if you ask me, that dude already won."

Even sadness over Spellman couldn't keep me from smiling. The mailman had no idea how right he was. Not to ruin the show for you, but the 11th contestant on "Who's Who?" is a waitress at an Italian restaurant in downtown Chicago. Eb found her.

26

By the time the two-hour season premiere of "Who's Who?" faded to a close, the sorority girls were frothing. Next Tuesday can't get here soon enough. They took turns declaring which of the guys on the show they are rooting for, as if that makes sense, and they spent the next hour gushing over every detail as to why. Most of them were pulling for Eb.

Their trips to the bar during the show were regular, adding a layer of drunken wandering to the conversation. Peg and I did our best to disregard the collective cackling.

"I don't get it," she said quietly, like there was any danger of offending the sorority girls. "Hard to believe what counts as entertainment these days."

I sipped my beer through a smile, enough to make it clear I shared the opinion.

Peg, when her serving responsibilities allowed, had been watching the show with idle curiosity. In two hours, the customer flow at the Nerdy Bird was surprisingly steady, and I had a front-row seat to witness the entire parade. By the time the show ended, the hunters were gone, probably already nearing their cabin in Kalkaska where they would plot the next day's blind-building mission in preparation for deer season. Peg got the stories of everybody, even those who didn't have a story to tell. As she stood there filling a pitcher of beer for a tall man with oil stains on his coveralls, she listened with feigned interest as he described a restoration project of an old '42 Continental. Spellman would have loved hearing about that.

I killed time by watching a 75-year-old man named Gus who sat two stools away, lazily carving something on the bar top with his car key. He'd been at it for quite a while, and I stole occasional peeks, anxious to see what he was writing. Or, rather, drawing. I still couldn't tell. Gus worked much more slowly in carving than he did in drinking.

"Hi Dan."

The words came in the form of a squeak from behind me, from the mouth of the little blonde girl whose name I never did hear. They all knew my name though. Funny.

"Hi," I replied, spinning to face her. "How'd you like the show?"

"It was Uh-," pause, "-Mazing!"

A handful of drinks had slowed her pace of speaking. But not much.

"We were just wondering, if it's not too much trouble, if you could, like, ask Ebner to send a photo to the sorority house," she said, letting her eyes drift across the bar top as she talked. "We were hoping maybe he could, like, autograph it. Or something. You know, if it's not too much trouble."

I didn't say anything at first, just smiled.

"Do you think you could ask him?"

I promised her I would, and her smile opened into a grotesque gash that let loose another piercing shriek.

"Awesome, thank you so much," she said. "Do you think you'll be talking to him soon?"

I assured her I would. Peg returned and was watching the entire exchange, her lips smiling as they wrapped around the straw of her Diet Coke and lime. We shared a glance before I returned to the blonde girl.

"I might even see him soon," I said, leaving out details of the after-party I was missing. "Why don't you write down the address of the sorority house and I'll make sure he gets it."

With that news, she returned to the group and a chorus of "OMIGOD"s filled the bar. Peg chuckled while refilling a glass of straws. Gus was still scratching away at his artwork. With the TV show over, Peg cut the volume and returned the juke box to its typical level, loud enough to fill a wooden cube of a neighborhood bar in the middle of cornfields and farmhouses and thick northern Michigan forests.

"So you might be seeing Ebner soon, huh?" she asked over the music as she wiped hardened ketchup from the tips of a tray of squeeze bottles. "Is that where you're heading? Chicago?"

I shrugged. She eyed me suspiciously, probably leery because of that lie I had told her earlier. I still regret that one.

"Mainly I just wanted to get away from town, at least for a little while," I said. "I didn't plan to be sitting here this long. There's a party tonight down in Chicago, Eb said he could get me in. I was thinking about going."

"But you weren't sure?" Peg asked. "You just got in your car and started driving?"

I nodded.

Peg couldn't understand someone getting in their car and driving without a destination, the same way she couldn't understand a bunch of college girls getting all riled up about a reality TV show.

"So what are you going to do now?" she asked.

I thought about it for a second.

"Like I said earlier," I said. "I guess I'll take pictures for a newspaper."

A concerned look replaced the carefree grin on Peg's face.

"What is it you're stuck on, honey?"

I glanced at Gus, who might have been listening as he carved. I didn't care.

"Remember Jim Gold, the guy whose wife just had the baby?" I asked. "He told me one night that people are either running to something or they're running away from something."

Peg returned to working at a clump of ketchup with her fingernail.

"And you don't agree with him?" she said.

"Not sure. I was just thinking about Spellman."

"What about?"

"If what Jim said is true, I was just wondering if Spellman, when he moved here from Colorado, was running to something, or running away from something."

Peg smiled to herself.

"Honey, if you ask me, your friend Jim might be right, but it doesn't matter," she said. "People run. Maybe to, maybe from. Or maybe both. It doesn't really matter. What matters is whether a person realizes what it is they're running to or from. And something tells me your boss did."

With that, Peg winked, spun and disappeared into the kitchen, balancing that tray of ketchup bottles in one hand and nudging the door with the other. I tucked a $20 bill under my empty beer glass and left, remembering to fold the napkin with the sorority house address in my wallet. Eb and I might want that someday.

The night sky was a speckled field of black broken only by a large, white-yellow moon that hung overhead. After a few hours in the bar, the cool air felt refreshing on my face. For the next hour, the parking lot outside the Nerdy Bird was quiet aside from occasional cars pulling in or out, the constant muffle of music that wrestled through the log-cabin walls, and a wall of cricket songs that lifted from the forest. The sorority girls finally spilled out of the bar in a giggling swarm, but thankfully they didn't see me in the shadows beyond the light of that sign for "Vennison Burgers."

I stood at the edge of the lot, where gravel meets pavement, and looked north and then south and then north again at 37 stretching both ways into the darkness. Staring into the black, I saw faces. Spellman, years ago driving this same span of road, leaving behind one life to discover a new one. Darren Morrell watching the premiere of "Who's Who?" from his hospital bed, fighting the ache of surgery and wondering about opportunity lost. Tyler Brennan, his knife nipping delicately at the meat of an apple. Jim Gold hovering over that paw print in the sand, the water of the Rustic River gliding behind it.

And then I walked to my car and imagined the new life waiting for me at the *Mirror*. As I pulled from the parking lot onto the highway, I heard Eb from the empty passenger seat. *"Don't do nothing, you'll regret it. Do something."* So I did. I pressed the accelerator, calculated the miles between me and Wanishing and watched the world slide by as the black of the national forest began its beautiful blur outside the windows. I've always liked it that way.

ABOUT THE AUTHOR

Born and raised in southeast Michigan, Ken Welsch studied journalism and creative writing at Central Michigan University in Mt. Pleasant, a campus and town that served as the inspirational blueprint for the fictional Great Lakes University and Wanishing in *Forever Since An Apple*.

He currently lives in suburban Detroit with his wife, Jenny, and their three children, Jason, Drew and Megan.

Made in the USA
Middletown, DE
14 July 2015